Slap!

Then . . . crying.

'Come here,' the Doctor ordered.

'Please . . .'

'Lift up your skirt.'

There was another moment of silence, and then the Girl let out an uncomfortable sound. 'Please, you're hurting me—'

'Shut *up*! . . . Look, there – he ejaculated.'

The Girl made no reply, only another uncomfortable sound.

'Do not make me do this again. Do you understand?'

'Yes, Doctor.'

There was silence. No more conversation. Just the sound of footsteps walking away down the hall.

The Adder did not move from the ladder. He stayed there, rooted to the spot like a gargoyle, and replayed the dialogue in his head. Over and over again. And a strange feeling rose up inside him. One he didn't like. The Doctor was stirring things up. Old things within him. Bad things. *Feelings*.

It was the Doctor's fault.

Like a distant, growing thunder, the laughter started in the Adder's head. And he closed his eyes, as if this would somehow shut out the sounds. Before they could expand on him again – before they could crash down on him like cold lightning – he climbed back down the ladder, opened up the dumbwaiter, and grabbed his recording equipment from the shelves. He shoved it all into a burlap sack, along with a drill, screw-gun and some screws.

Then, with the burlap sack slung around his shoulder, the Adder crouched down low and climbed inside the dumbwaiter. He then began climbing up the old chute, one bracket at a time. He headed for the second floor.

For the room that was forbidden.

Sixty-Seven

Striker and Felicia spent the next half-hour checking out the rest of Metrotown Mall, but Striker knew in his heart it would be a wasted effort. Larisa had seen Bernard Hamilton of Car 87, and she had hightailed it as far from Burnaby South as her legs would carry her.

Their one big chance, destroyed.

While Felicia did another run around of the main level, Striker attended the security office and spoke to the two guards inside. He emailed the office a copy of Larisa's picture and told them to scour the footage and see if they could find her.

He had little hope of success.

By the time he was done and leaving the small office, Felicia was already outside waiting for him. She had two cups of Tim Horton's coffee in her hands and a tired but determined look on her face. Striker took one of the paper cups from her, said thanks.

'Any luck?' he asked, already knowing the answer.

'She's gone,' was all Felicia said.

Striker could not help but scowl as they headed back to the car. 'This is such bullshit,' he griped. 'That fuckin' Bernard. He's royally screwed it for us on this one.'

Felicia nodded. 'I wonder who his source is.'

Striker took a sip of his coffee. It was too sweet. As usual, Felicia had put sugar in it. 'There is no source,' he said. 'Never was.'

'Then how—'

'Hamilton was eavesdropping on our conversation when we went over the air,' he said. 'He heard you on Dispatch, then he listened in when we switched to Info and requested a Burnaby unit to attend here. He caught on. Figured out we were coming for Larisa.'

'You really think? That's pretty devious.'

'I know it is, and I know Bernard.' Striker thought of how they had also coincidentally run into Bernard at 312 Main Street when checking for warrants. There were too many coincidences with the man. He turned to Felicia. 'Run a history of Bernard's unit status. I'll bet you a hundred bucks he was closer than we were when we made the call to Burnaby. It's how he got on scene so fast.'

Felicia grabbed the computer and ran the Remote Log. After a few seconds, she nodded. 'You're right, he was already out here at the same time we made the call. He put himself out at Boundary and Adanac Street.'

Striker glanced over at her. 'Recognize the location?'

'Mapleview,' she said.

'Exactly. He was probably there looking for Larisa. Or trying to get information.'

'But why? Why would he care so much?'

Striker gave her a bemused look. 'You still don't get it, do you? Bernard *doesn't* care. When was the last time you saw him put in this kind of work for any other mentally ill patient?'

'Well, never.'

'Exactly. Bernard just wants to be the one to *save* Larisa. Think about it. She's a former employee of the Vancouver Police Department. A Victim Services worker, no less. And she's been through hell and back. Now Bernard Hamilton – caring community cop and all-around godsend – comes along and rescues her from her mental illness. Think of how he'd spin that one.'

Felicia nodded. 'More glory in his bid for Cop of the Year.'

'Exactly. The worst part is he knows he's actually putting her in greater danger – and ruining our chances of getting her back safely. But he doesn't care. Because he wants to be the one who scores on the arrest.' Striker felt his entire body grow tight with anger. 'He'll never get that award. Not ever. Because everyone knows what he's all about. He doesn't care about Larisa or any of them.'

'He cares about the publicity,' Felicia said.

'He wants publicity, I'll make sure he gets some,' Striker said. 'Starting off within the department.'

Felicia gave him a curious look, and he smiled at her darkly.

'Later,' he told her. 'When the time is right.'

A half-hour later, at exactly eight o'clock, they drove back over Boundary Road municipal border and entered the City of Vancouver.

'We're looking at this the wrong way,' Striker said. 'Let's stop trying to find out *where* Larisa went and find out *why*.'

Felicia gave him an odd look. 'We already know why.'

'Do we?' he asked.

'The medical warrant.'

He shook his head. 'There's something else she's running from here, something besides the medical warrant. There has to be. Think about it. The woman emailed me and told me she believed Mandy was murdered. She also had Sarah's name written down in her place. At the time, we thought it was all part of her mental illness. But now I wonder.'

Felicia nodded. 'It was almost like she had proof.'

Striker thought of all the opened DVD cases they had found on the floor of Larisa's ransacked rancher.

'We need to find out what that proof was,' he said.

Felicia opened up the laptop with a renewed sense of energy about her. 'Let's go over everything one more time.'

Striker pulled over to the side of the road. He opened up his notebook, then the file folder of all the evidence he had collected back at Larisa's rancher. There was a ton of stuff. Stories. Articles. Newspaper clippings.

One thing stuck out more than all the rest. It was the article from the Vancouver *Province* newspaper about the man who committed suicide at the Regency Hotel. Someone had used a thick pen to write *LIES! LIES! LIES!* across it.

Striker read through the article, saw that the victim's name was Derrick Smallboy. The man was said to have suffered from depression, addiction and fetal alcohol syndrome.

A hell of a trio.

Striker found the article intriguing, in a dark sort of way. 'Run this name,' he said to Felicia. 'Derrick Smallboy. Age twenty-eight.'

She did, and after a moment the feed came back.

'He's deceased,' she said.

'I know that; he's the guy from this article. Read up on him, tell me what you find.'

Felicia did. After a long moment, she looked up with a shocked look on her face. 'Holy shit, Jacob, look at this. Says here that Smallboy suffered from depression, FAS, alcoholism, and schizophrenia. This guy was really messed up. He ended up throwing himself off the top of the Regency Hotel.'

'I know all that.'

'Be patient,' she told him, and read on. 'Says here he was enrolled in the EvenHealth programme, and was taking SILC classes.'

That made Striker take notice.

He leaned over and scanned through the report. As he learned

the basics – that Derrick Smallboy had plummeted from the top of the Regency Hotel with no witnesses and no evidence of foul play – something else caught his eye.

A Lost Property file where Smallboy was listed as a complainant.

'Bring up that one,' he said.

Felicia exited the current report and brought up the Lost Property page. The synopsis was brief. Smallboy had lost several pieces of ID, namely his BC driver's licence, his status card, and his birth certificate. He believed they had been stolen, but the author of the report hinted at paranoia.

'Go back into Larisa's main page again,' Striker said.

When Felicia did, he pointed to one of the reports Larisa had made in August last year. It was listed as a Lost Property report, and when Felicia brought up the synopsis, he saw the same basic facts.

All of Larisa's ID had been taken. Just like Smallboy's. She also thought it had been stolen. But there was no proof of this. Not even a possible suspect. In the end, the report had been cleared as Unfounded.

Striker looked at Felicia. 'You still have your contact at Equifax?'

'You bet. TransUnion, too.'

'Call them. Find out if there were any credit problems with Smallboy and Larisa.'

Felicia got on the phone and got hold of her contact at the credit bureau who could search both TransUnion and Equifax databases. The process was slow and cumbersome, but after almost twenty minutes, she hung up the phone with a curious look on her face.

'Bad credit reports?' Striker asked.

'The worst. Non-payments. R3s. You name it. And it gets

worse than that,' she said. 'Smallboy and Logan were both victims of identity theft. Full frauds. It's all documented with the bureau. Someone damn well bankrupted them. Took out credit cards in their names, emptied their bank accounts – everything.'

Striker felt the energy of a new lead.

'Awfully coincidental,' he said.

'That's not the half of it,' Felicia continued. 'I also got him to check on Mandy Gill and Sarah Rose. Exact same thing. They *all* had their IDs stolen and they were *all* victims of identity theft.'

'Did Larisa report the physical theft of the identification, or that someone was using her identity to obtain more credit?' he clarified.

'Both.'

Striker looked down at the date when Larisa Logan had reported the identity theft.

'Larisa made a report of this on August third of last year,' he noted.

Felicia nodded. 'And three days later, she was committed.'

'To where?'

'Riverglen.'

'By whose order?' Striker asked.

'Dr Riley M. Richter.'

Striker leaned back against the seat, his head swirling with information. Four victims of identity theft. All connected through the doctors of the EvenHealth programme. And now three of them were dead, one was missing.

The odds were astronomical.

'It all comes back to the doctors,' he said. 'To Ostermann and Richter.'

He'd barely finished speaking the words when his cell phone

rang. He picked it up, stuck it to his ear, and said, 'Detective Striker, Homicide.'

The voice responding was smooth and soft. *Feminine*.

'This is Dr Richter. Apparently you've been looking for me.'

Sixty-Eight

The address Dr Richter gave Striker was for a road named Stone Creek Slope in West Vancouver, Canada's most expensive area of real estate. Within ten seconds of driving off the Trans-Canada Highway and entering the district, Striker could see why.

The lots became large and more secluded. Driveways were flanked by tall rows of old-growth cedars, and most of the mansions were barely visible behind the gated driveways and high stone walls. Every house had a veranda that stared out over the cold deep waters of the strait below.

Striker looked out over those waterways. They appeared like polished black stone, matching the cloudless night sky. Beyond them was the city of Vancouver, all lit up and busy. Just another weekday night in a city buzzing with night life.

He drove slowly down the long swerving slope of hill, until he spotted the address they were looking for on the left. A small driveway compared to the others, almost hidden by the trees.

'It feels so secluded out here,' Felicia said. 'Like we're out in the middle of nowhere — yet the city's just a ten-minute drive away. It's beautiful.'

'And costs a fortune. That's why only doctors and lawyers and celebrities live here.'

He turned the car up the driveway and stopped on a small, round parking area. They got out. The house before them was not as plush as the others but, in this neighbourhood, 'not plush' still meant worth millions.

Out front, the alcove lights suddenly turned on and the front door opened. Standing in the doorway was a woman of maybe thirty years, dressed in a sombre black dress jacket and matching skirt. She had soft brown hair that was long, but tied up in a bun. A strong but pretty face. And confident eyes that held Striker's gaze without a moment's nervousness.

'Good evening,' she said. 'I'm Dr Richter. I've been expecting you.'

Moments later, after they were all inside and introductions had been made, they moved into a small sunken den that overlooked the pool area outside and, beyond that, the cliffs over the strait. On the coffee table was a bowl of ripe mandarin oranges. The smell of them filled the room.

Striker sat down in a leather EZ Boy recliner, directly across from Dr Richter, who took the loveseat. In between them, on a matching sofa, sat Felicia.

'Nice place,' Striker offered.

Dr Richter tucked one leg under the other and smoothed out her skirt. 'It's my uncle's,' she replied. 'The rent is good and he lives just across the street, which is perfect for me since I'm away much of the time. He keeps an eye on things for me.'

'Were you away yesterday?' Striker asked. 'I left you several messages.'

'Yes, and I apologize for not getting back to you sooner. I hadn't bothered to check my messages since the day before. And then, all day long, I was flying back from New York.'

'Conference?' Felicia asked.

Dr Richter shook her head. 'I have family out there. I visited a little bit, did the mandatory social thing. But I was really there to assess the area. I'm considering opening a private practice there. The money is triple what I can make here, and the taxes less than half.'

'That's quite a difference,' Felicia remarked.

'It's a difference of fifteen years – retiring at fifty versus sixty-five.' Dr Richter gave them both a quick look, then spoke again. 'I didn't get into this profession for the love of psychiatry,' she said bluntly. 'I entered this field to make a lot of money, to retire young and still enjoy life.'

'And yet you choose to work for EvenHealth,' Striker pointed out.

'Yes,' she admitted, as if not making the connection.

He explained. 'They're government subsidized, and Dr Ostermann has built his reputation on helping out the poorest of patients. I'm sure the government don't pay anywhere near what the private practices pay – especially in this area.'

'They don't,' Dr Richter replied. 'I'm not working at EvenHealth for the money, I'm there for the experience. Dr Ostermann's name reaches to far places. Plus, I wanted to see how he had put together the programme. My goal in New York is to start my own private programme with doctors working *for me*. That's where the money is.'

Striker found the woman interesting. Blunt and brutally honest, but interesting. Charming, even. He pulled out his notebook and leafed back through the pages until he came to what he was looking for.

'You prescribed medications to some patients,' he began. 'Exact same kind and dosage.' He reached out to show her what

he had written in his notebook; she read the names and medications listed on the page.

'These patients, were they part of EvenHealth?' she asked.

'Yes. Enrolled in the SILC classes.'

Dr Richter made an *ahh* sound. 'The group sessions. Social Independence and Life Coping skills.' She smiled. 'One of Dr Ostermann's ten-step programmes. It is aimed primarily at bipolar patients, for the most. A few of the patients have Generalized Anxiety Disorder. Lexapro and Effexor are common treatments for this. They more often than not work extremely well, especially when taken together. For any more detail than that, I'd have to check my files.'

'You don't recognize your own prescriptions?' Striker asked.

Dr Richter laughed bemusedly. 'Detective, please. Between my work with EvenHealth and the other clinics, I've treated over seven hundred patients in the last year. Each one of them is on as many as ten different medications. That's *seven thousand* medications in total. Do you honestly think I remember them all?'

'Sounds like mass production.'

'It sounds like *money*,' she said brazenly. 'I've already told you, I never joined this profession for the long hours and the constant lack of progress, I joined it to make money. Cold, hard cash. And I intend on being retired on a beach in Jamaica by the time I'm forty.'

Striker ignored that. 'I'm less concerned about the medication types and more concerned about the patient names,' Striker said. 'Mandy Gill, Sarah Rose, and Larisa Logan, in particular.'

Dr Richter said nothing for a moment. Her eyes took on a faraway look and her face remained expressionless. In that moment, she looked older. And much more experienced. *Clinical*.

'I have a vague recollection of the group,' she finally said. 'And I'm not overly comfortable discussing them, especially not without perusing the file first – remember, I was only a fill-in for the group when Dr Ostermann could not be present.'

'Larisa Logan,' he pressed.

Dr Richter gave him a cold look, but then spoke anyway. 'Her, I do remember. She was a Victim Services worker, if I recall correctly.'

'She was,' Striker confirmed. 'Her family was killed in a car accident. She suffered a breakdown.'

'Yes, I remember Larisa Logan. She was a kind and genuine person. I felt for her.'

Striker doubted that, but said nothing.

'Larisa is missing,' Felicia interjected. 'And we're desperate to find her – not for any criminal reasons, but for her own safety.'

Dr Richter's face took on a confused look. 'I don't understand, why are you here talking to me?'

Striker blinked. 'Are you not her doctor?'

'No. Not at all. As I already explained, I was only an *interim* doctor for the SILC classes. I never worked with any of the patients during private sessions – there's no money there.'

'Then who was Larisa's doctor?' Felicia asked.

'Why, Dr Ostermann, of course.'

Striker leaned forward in his chair. 'Let me get this straight here. Other than the odd fill-in day here and there, you never worked with Larisa?'

'Of course not. She was Dr Ostermann's patient, and his alone. He was quite . . . possessive of her, really. His own personal project.'

Striker looked at Felicia and saw the tightness of her expression. He steered the conversation back to other matters – whether Dr Richter had ever used any experimental medication on the

patients, whether she had any connections to the army, and whether she ever did any work at Riverglen Mental Health Facility.

The answer to all three questions was a resounding *no*.

When they were done with the interview, Striker stood up and put his notebook away. He shook the woman's hand, and thanked her for her time. Then, with Felicia at his side, he walked to the front door.

'Keep your phone nearby,' he said to Dr Richter. 'I have a feeling I'll be calling you again.'

'Any time,' she replied.

But no smile parted her lips.

They drove back out of the cedar-covered hills of West Vancouver and took the highway to the downtown core. During the drive, Striker tried to relax his mind and let everything fall into place. But Felicia was unusually wired.

'We have the connection,' she said. 'Dr Ostermann was seeing *all four* patients – Gill, Rose, Mercury and Larisa Logan – and he was seeing them not only during group sessions but one-on-one.'

Striker nodded. 'I agree. He's also about the same size and stature as the man who attacked me back at the Gill crime scene – but it's all still circumstantial at this point. Everything.'

Felicia scowled. 'Which means what, he gets a free ride?'

'No. Which means we see the man.'

Felicia nodded, but her face took on a concerned look. 'Just be careful you don't tip him off on anything.'

Striker gave her a quick glance as they headed over the Lions Gate Bridge. 'I said *see* him, not speak to him.' He took out his cell phone and dialled Hans Jager – *Meathead*, to anyone who knew him. Meathead was one of the breachers for the Emergency

Response Team. The man answered, they talked, and a few minutes later, Striker hung up the phone and headed for the Cambie Street bridge.

There was some equipment they needed to pick up.

Sixty-Nine

The Adder had no idea what time it was when he finished the set-up. It could have been eight o'clock at night, it could have been well into the morning hours. He did not know. He did not care. Time held little importance to him, and he only took careful note of it when on a mission. All that mattered now was that the set-up was complete. And that it was done well.

It was.

The bulk of the camera's body sat within the steel bracket, which was screwed securely to the two-by-four beams of the dumbwaiter. The lens poked through the small hole in the wall, coming flush with the other side – just a one-inch lens that focused on the centre part of the Doctor's private room.

The forbidden room.

The Adder turned on the camera and looked at the LED screen. The image displayed was angled perfectly. It captured the oak bureau across the room. The four-poster king-sized bed in the centre of the room. The locked cabinet in the far corner.

The camera took in *everything*.

As if scripted, the Doctor returned, and not alone. At first the Adder reared from the camera and started to make his way back down the long and narrow chute of the dumbwaiter. But something made him pause.

A dark curiosity.

He climbed back to the top and stared at the camera's LED screen. Already the motion sensor had been triggered and the recording had been started. The two people in the room were beginning. The Adder had heard the act before. He had seen the results. He had known it existed.

But he had never actually *seen* it.

Now, as he stood in the darkness and watched the Doctor unlock the cabinet, a strange feeling invaded his chest. And it only got worse when he saw what the Doctor pulled out.

He should have felt shock. Fear. Revulsion. He should have felt all of these things, he knew, but he felt none of them. All he experienced was a growing tension in his chest, one that spread all throughout his core as he watched the LED screen in near disbelief.

When the screams began and the first glimpse of blood appeared, the Adder wanted to leave the chute, but he did not. He stayed there, fixated, immobile. A statue in the dark.

He just could not take his eyes away.

Seventy

The traffic was surprisingly bad, so they were later than antici-
pated. Striker half expected Meathead to be gone by the time
they reached the north end of the Cambie Street bridge. But
within seconds of reaching the bottom of Nelson Street, Felicia
spotted a group of big men clad in black jump suits. In the heavy
darkness of the night, they blended well. Most of them were
climbing into a white van that was parked kerbside.

They were ERT. The Emergency Response Team.

Canada's answer to SWAT.

The cluster of cops were Red Team, and Striker knew most of
them: Reid Noble, who everyone called Jitters. Davey Combs,
who was only five foot six but over two hundred and twenty
pounds of muscle. And Victor Santos, who was a crazy-ass
bastard and – thank God – no relation to Felicia. Their sergeant,
Zulu 51, was Tyrone Takuto, a top-notch Eurasian cop Striker
had known and respected for years. He would be Chief one day.
Striker knew it.

All the men looked tired from training, but happy to be going.
It was Miller time.

Striker parked on Nelson and scanned the street both ways.
'You see Meathead anywhere?'

'Just in my nightmares,' Felicia said.

Striker laughed at that. She had barely spoken the words

when they looked up at the nearest skyscraper and spotted the man. Meathead was rappelling down the south side of the building. He was three storeys up and still looked massive. At six foot four and two hundred and seventy pounds, he was a force to be reckoned with.

He saw Striker from the second storey level and gave a holler. When his eyes found Felicia, a large smile spread his lips and he yelled out, 'Hey, honey-cakes, can I come down there and butter your muffin?'

'Butter *this*!' she called back.

Meathead let out a hoarse laugh, then rappelled down to ground level. He tried to lever down, did it a bit too fast, and accidentally unclipped before his feet were fully planted. He fell awkwardly, landing half on his ass, half on his hands.

'Smooth,' Felicia said.

Meathead looked up and grinned. 'I always fall for the hotties.'

She made an *ugh* sound.

'I was referring to Shipwreck.'

Meathead let out a hyena laugh and climbed to his feet. Striker was six foot one and two hundred and twenty pounds. No small man. And yet next to Meathead, he felt under-sized. He moved up to the breacher, and the two bantered about their old partnership days for a few minutes. Then Meathead packed up his gear and started placing it in the transport van.

'About the gear,' Striker said.

Meathead nodded. 'Yeah, yeah. I got what you need right here, but you got to get it back to me tonight or Stark will have my balls in a sling.'

Striker nodded. James Stark was the inspector in charge of the Emergency Response Team. He was a by-the-book guy and would never have allowed Striker the gear he wanted without

the proper paperwork – and even then, probably not. ERT was his baby, and he liked to keep it separate.

Meathead was sticking his neck out for them on this one, and Striker appreciated it.

'Scout's honour,' he said.

Meathead just gave him a look like he didn't fully believe him. Still he grabbed two pairs of night vision binoculars from his gear bag. He handed one to Striker, and Striker took it. When Felicia reached for hers, Meathead held them up to his eyes, looked at her chest, and said, 'Yummy.'

'Give me the goddam binocs,' she said.

When Meathead held them out again, she snatched them away from him. She gave Striker a hard look and said, 'I still think we should be getting SF for this.'

SF. Strike Force. The Vancouver Police Surveillance Team.

Striker frowned. Felicia had already brought up the topic in the car and, as usual, she was refusing to let the issue go.

'We can do this ourselves,' he said.

'We're not trained for it.'

'Trained?' He laughed. 'We're not going mobile, we're just setting up a stake-out. Like a drug buy. God, how many of those have you done?'

Felicia just shrugged. She'd probably done over a hundred in her time.

'We're just making observations,' Striker said.

'SF is still the best way to go.'

'And SF will take *time*,' he argued. 'Time to write up the forms. Time to make the requests. Time for them to be read over and approved. And you know as well as I do that Laroche does *nothing* out of policy.'

Felicia said nothing for a long moment, then looked at her watch.

'It's getting late,' she said.

Striker agreed. He looked at Meathead. 'I'll put these back in your locker when we're done.'

'Be sure you do,' he said. 'This is my ass on the line.'

Striker said nothing more. He took the gear with him and stuffed it in the trunk. When Felicia returned to the car, they hopped inside and got going. It was going on for nine o'clock now, and there was no time to waste.

The Endowment Lands were only ten minutes away.

The Ostermann house was on Belmont Avenue.

Striker parked a few blocks out and they went in on foot, coming in from the west. When they reached the lot, Striker slowed down. Inside the gated entrance, the house sat with most of the lights turned off. Only a few were left on – the ones in the library and kitchen, most noticeably.

'Looks like no one's home,' Felicia said.

Striker pointed to the Land Rover parked beside the house and the BMW in the drive. 'Someone's home.'

He assessed the house. The rooms that interested him the most – the master bedroom, the office and what appeared to be the study – were all located on the southwest side. That made the small grove of Japanese plum trees the best vantage point for surveillance. There was a small elevation there, near that corner of the yard, and the area was dark.

'Over there,' he suggested.

'I already see it,' Felicia said.

Striker looked at the neighbouring lot, the one to the east. There were no dogs. No sign of people. And all the lights in the house were off, as if the owners were away for the night.

It was the perfect place for entry.

Gear in hand, they made their way into the neighbouring lot.

All down the yard, a stone-and-cement wall separated the two properties. When they were a third of the way down, in behind the tall, bony Japanese plum trees, Striker stopped. He checked his cell phone to be sure it was set on vibrate, then looked at Felicia.

'Make sure your ringer is off.'

She did.

Satisfied, he assessed the wall. It was eight feet high, so he had to give Felicia a boost over. Once she was there, he took a running start, sprung up off the wall and pulled himself over behind her.

In the Ostermann yard everything was quiet and still. From the grassy elevation they knelt on, the entire south and east sides of the mansion could be seen. Between the trees to the north, Striker could see past the end of the floodlit yard to the cliffs beyond. Out in the strait, the moon shimmered off the waves and made the water look like smoked glass.

'We can see the bedroom, den and study from here,' Felicia noted. 'But the library and kitchen are completely out of view.'

Striker nodded. 'Then go around back. See if you can find a different vantage point for the kitchen and library. When you get one, call me. That way we'll have the whole house covered.'

Felicia climbed to her feet and slowly made her way down the east side of the house. When she turned the corner, she was blocked from sight by the barbecue area. With her out of sight, Striker took out his binocs and used them to focus in on the front of the house.

In the driveway was Dr Ostermann's BMW. Parked at the east side of the house was the Land Rover. Striker looked past it, past the stone-and-steel pillars of the driveway and the

old-fashioned lanterns that lined the cobblestone walkways. He focused on the window to the doctor's study.

The blind was drawn, the drapes pulled shut behind it.

His cell vibrated against his side, so he snatched it up and brought it to his ear.

'I have a good position,' Felicia said. 'I can see the entire north and west sides of the house.'

'Anything of interest?'

Felicia made an unhappy sound. 'The place looks empty.'

'Just keep watching. And be ready to go at a moment's notice.'

He hung up and looked at the house.

For a long moment, he watched the study, staring at the blind as if it would suddenly pop open and reveal to him the secrets that lay behind it. It didn't, of course, and after a few more minutes, Striker placed his focus on the office below. It appeared vacant. All the lights were off. There was no movement inside.

He looked at the master bedroom. There the drapes were only half pulled shut, but with the telescopic lens of the binocs he could see inside.

Everything there was just as dark and still as the office.

He was just about to reposition himself to be more comfortable, when the bedroom door opened and the light flicked on. Walking in through the door was Dr Ostermann – although walking seemed an odd word for it. He moved gingerly, limping more than walking. And when he began to take off his shirt, the action clearly pained him. He slid the shirt off his body and let it drop to the floor.

As Striker watched the man, he noticed a few long reddish marks. Scratch marks maybe. One ran down the side of the man's neck and one trailed across the top of his back. He tried to focus in for a better look, but the doctor stepped out of view and remained hidden behind the partly closed curtains.

Striker remembered how gingerly the man had moved the first time he had met him – just hours after the suspect had fought with him and jumped out of the third-storey window of Mandy Gill's building.

Now, here he was, seemingly injured again.

It was strange.

The thought had barely formed in his mind when the front door suddenly swung open. From the house ran Dalia. She had her hands over her ears and her face was tight. She raced across the front yard, opened the gate, and then ran down Belmont Avenue to the west. When she reached the next lot, Striker lost sight of her.

Something was wrong.

Striker took out his cell and called Felicia. 'You getting anything back there?'

'Nothing. All dead.'

'Well, I got the doctor in view, and he looks like he's been in a fight again. Plus, Dalia just went racing out of the house like it was on fire. Something's going on here, Feleesh. I'm moving in for a closer look.'

'Let's get another unit here first.'

'This will just take a second.'

'There's something weird about this family, Jacob. I don't like it. It's not safe.'

'No police work is.'

'This is different.'

'Just cover me, Feleesh. Cover me and keep your radio turned on.'

He hung up the phone, got up from his prone position and made his way through the plum trees. As he reached the driveway and roundabout, he tucked the binoculars inside his inner coat pocket, then made his way up the steps of the front walkway.

The front door was half open, and everything inside the mansion was quiet and still. Down at the far end of the hall, the lights from the kitchen and library were on, flooding the area with bone-yellow light.

No one was there.

Striker stepped inside the foyer. The air felt hot compared to outside, and the soft hum of the furnace filled his ears.

'Hello?' he called out.

No response.

He leaned back outside and hit the doorbell. Loud chimes rang through the house, echoing in the foyer. Moments later, the sound of footsteps could be heard, stomping across the hard-wood floor above.

Master bedroom, Striker deemed.

He waited patiently as the footsteps grew louder, until Dr Ostermann appeared at the top of the stairs. Even from a floor away, the beads of sweat on the man's skin were noticeable, as was the heavy breathing of his chest. His dark eyes were acute and flitted constantly around the foyer, even if his body moved lethargically. He took one step down the mahogany staircase and, upon seeing Striker, came to a sudden stop.

'Detective,' he said. He could not hide the surprise in his voice. 'This is rather . . . unexpected.'

'You and I need to talk.'

Dr Ostermann nodded slowly. 'Need to talk . . . Well, yes, of course. Why don't you drop by tomorrow morning and we—'

'Not tomorrow. *Now*,' Striker said.

He closed the door behind him.

Seventy-One

For some reason, the library was excessively hot and humid. Hot air blew in from the furnace ducts all around the room, strong and steady. Striker closed one of the vents with the toe of his shoe. As he looked around the room, he saw the Ostermann family's photographs on the mantel once more. Staring back at him were the pictures of Lexa and Dalia, Dr Ostermann and Gabriel. The first time Striker had come here, something about these pictures had bothered him. At the time, he didn't know what.

Now he understood.

It was the smiles. Each one near perfect, as if carved into their faces. But there were signs within those expressions of other emotions. The fear in Lexa Ostermann's eyes; the hollowness in Dalia's stare; and the way that Gabriel looked back, eyes acute and focused, the smile on his lips never causing a wrinkle near his eyes or brow.

It was all plastic.

Only the doctor looked truly happy, his smile stretching his goatee across his face. The rest of the family looked like they were all wearing masks. Striker wondered what was behind each one. As he considered this, Dr Ostermann stepped into the room behind him. His face looked tired and his slumped posture was no different.

'This is about Billy again, I would presume.'

Striker gestured towards the picture of Dalia. 'She's a beautiful girl.'

Dr Ostermann nodded, almost hesitantly. 'She is that. She is also stubborn and defiant and complicated.'

'How is her hearing?'

The doctor blinked. 'Her hearing? Why, it's fine, as far as I'm aware. Why do you ask?'

'Because she ran out of here like a bat outta hell, covering her ears. So I'm thinking either she's been hearing things she doesn't like, or there's a problem with her ears.'

Dr Ostermann's face turned slightly pink. 'What are you here for, Detective?'

'I came here to discuss some . . . *oddities* that keep popping up with Billy's case, but then when Dalia came racing out of the front door, I reconsidered.'

'I can assure you, Detective, you do not need to worry about Dalia.'

'I think I do.' Striker took a step closer to Dr Ostermann and gazed at the side of the man's neck. At the crimson bands in his flesh. 'Where'd you get those marks?'

Dr Ostermann's face reddened further. 'I hardly think that's any of your business.'

'Then we got a problem here, because I do think it's my business. In fact, I think it's my *duty*.' Striker took his hands from his coat pockets and explained. 'I got a girl racing out of here like the house is on fire, and I got you with marks up your neck and back, moving about with the sensitivity of a burn victim. All in all, it makes me ask myself: is everyone here all right?'

For a moment, Dr Ostermann's eyes took on a strange, panicked look, and Striker half expected the man to run. Or maybe even attack. But the doctor did none of this. Dr

Ostermann took a long look at him, as if to compose his thoughts, and then let out a jovial laugh.

'You think I'm abusing my family?' he asked.

'It crossed my mind.'

Dr Ostermann finally stopped chuckling, and when he did all humour left his face. 'You are quite the investigator, Detective Striker.' He pulled his collar away from his neck, so that Striker could better see the marks. 'It's called *shingles*.'

'Shingles?'

'Yes. Brought on by the herpes zoster virus. I'm sure you've heard of it before – the chicken pox virus.' When Striker said nothing back, Dr Ostermann continued. 'It usually only comes out when a person is at their weakest. Which, I guess, would make it my own fault. I've been working weeks of sixty and seventy hours for half a year now. Stress at Mapleview; stress at Riverglen – it's no wonder my body has become run-down. And then all the drama that was happening with Billy – well, I guess that was all it took to put me over the edge.'

'Shingles,' Striker said again.

Dr Ostermann nodded slowly. 'It's been a very unpleasant two days now. I have marks down my neck and back and waist – and I can hardly move. Even showering is painful.'

Striker said nothing back as he thought this over. 'And Dalia?' he asked.

Dr Ostermann sighed. 'Fighting her mother – as usual. Which is why I was upstairs in the first place. They're too much alike, those two, and when they get like that, it's best to just leave them alone. Retreat to a place of solace.'

'And where is your wife now then?'

'In the bath, I would think. She was drawing one when I heard the doorbell.' Dr Ostermann gave Striker a long look

before sighing. 'If you insist, I can get her out of the tub to come down here and talk to you.'

Striker ignored the comment and focused the conversation back on other matters. 'How long were you treating Mandy for?'

Dr Ostermann raised an eyebrow. 'We're changing subjects, I see. How long did I treat Mandy Gill for? I'm not sure. A couple of years, I would think.'

'And Sarah Rose?'

'About the same.'

'What about Billy?'

'I've been treating Billy ever since he came back from Afghanistan and was recommended to my programme, which would be about three years ago – is there a point to all this, Detective?'

'What about Larisa Logan? How long were you treating her?'

Dr Ostermann's face took on a look of understanding, and he nodded. 'I see now. Larisa. I'm afraid I can say little about her.'

'I know you were treating her.'

'I will neither confirm nor deny that.'

'You don't have to,' Striker said. 'I already have confirmation. I know that you were seeing all four patients – Mandy, Sarah, Billy *and* Larisa. Now three of them are dead and Larisa is missing. Does that not seem odd to you?'

Dr Ostermann gingerly sat down in one of the library chairs, letting out a tender sound as he did. 'Unfortunately, Detective, it does not. All it tells me is that I should have seen how danger-ous Billy was in the first place. It tells me that I failed at being his doctor and it cost two innocent people – maybe even three – their lives.'

Striker was unmoved. 'It tells me something else – that maybe I've been looking at the wrong person.'

Dr Ostermann's face had a lost expression; then it tightened

and turned pink. 'I understand your insinuation, Detective, and it is *not* appreciated.'

'I wouldn't think so.'

Dr Ostermann stood up from the chair. 'I think it's time you took your leave, sir. And when you return next time I should hope you have a warrant, for I will surely have spoken to my own counsel – criminal *and* civil. It would appear our friendly conversations are over.'

Striker nodded. 'That choice is entirely yours.'

When Dr Ostermann gestured towards the library exit, Striker took a long look around the room, purposely taking his time, then walked down the hall towards the front door. When he reached the foyer, he ran right into Lexa Ostermann.

'Detective Striker?' she said, surprised.

'Mrs Ostermann.'

She looked down at herself – at the revealing kimono she wore – and her cheeks blushed. She gestured upstairs, to the west side of the house. 'I'm sorry . . . I was getting into the bath . . . I thought you were Dalia coming back . . .'

'Do not speak to him,' Dr Ostermann said, coming up behind them.

Lexa's face took on a confused look.

Striker ignored the man. He nodded to Lexa, then moved to the front door. Once there, he turned around and looked at them. Dr Ostermann stood in the forefront, his face hard as rock, his fingers curled into fists. Behind him, on the first step, stood Lexa. Her cheeks were rosy with blush and her deep brown eyes looked uncertain beneath the long, blonde curls of hair that fell across her brow.

Shingles? Striker thought.

He thought of how he and Felicia had almost burned up in that fire. And he remembered the camera set up outside the

window, facing in through the iron-barred panes of glass, capturing their demise. It angered him, and he felt like grabbing the doctor right there. Snapping him in two. Instead, he gave the man a long, hard look and smiled. 'One last thing you might be interested in, Dr Ostermann . . . I know all about your videos.'

The angry, smug look fell from Dr Ostermann's face and was replaced by a pale sick expression.

Lexa looked at her husband. 'What videos? What is he talking about?'

Dr Ostermann said nothing. He reached out, and with a trembling hand opened the front door. 'Goodnight, Detective.'

'Not for you, it won't be.'

Striker walked through the front door and never looked back.

Seventy-Two

The Adder was sitting on the cold concrete floor, in his Place of Solace, thinking of nothing when he heard the loud angry *shrenk!* of the hatch being opened. Had he not locked it? He turned around oddly from his seated position, surprised by the familiar sound, and slowly slid the DVD – his most precious of all the precious videos – into the inner pocket of his coat. Then he looked back up towards the hatch.

Clambering down the ladder was the Doctor.

This surprised the Adder, for no one ever came down here. *No one.* Not in ten years. This room had always been his, and his alone. Having the hatch opened at all was an intrusion.

He climbed to his feet and turned around.

The Doctor reached the bottom of the ladder. 'You taped it? You taped it, didn't you? You stupid, stupid *fool*!'

'I don't know what you're talking about.'

'Don't lie *to me*!'

SMACK!

The Adder felt his head jolt to the left and he reeled backwards, his cheek hot and stinging. For a moment, he did nothing. He just stood there in the centre of the room and felt the air hum about him. Felt that feeling wash over him once more. And suddenly he was fading again. Melting away into that other

place. And the sounds started to come back, starting with the high-pitched laughter.

'I need some space,' he found himself saying. 'I'm losing control.'

The Doctor paid him no attention and instead found the box of DVDs on the floor. With one quick swoop, they were taken away.

And just like that the Adder couldn't breathe.

'No,' he managed to get out.

'You can't have these.'

'They're mine.'

'I'm destroying them.'

'No, they're mine! They're *mine*!'

The Adder felt his entire body begin to shake, so hard the room wobbled and vibrated all around him.

As always, the Doctor paid him no heed. Just ignored him. Climbed back up the ladder. And took away the videos of everything the Adder held precious in life. Everything the Adder loved. Everything the Adder needed to calm the frantic voices in his head and keep himself rooted in the reality of this cold and horrible world.

The hatch slammed shut.

And then he was alone again.

Just him and the voices.

'No,' he said softly, and then there was a desperation in his voice even he could hear. 'NO!'

The voices came at him in waves. Thunderous, overpowering waves. And the Adder did the only thing he could do. He gave in and let the voices take him away. And after that he remembered nothing.

Seventy-Three

Striker exited the front walkway of the lot, rounded the corner on to the sidewalk and continued east until he was out of view. He then ran back down the side of the neighbour's lot, climbed the wall and dropped down next to Felicia under the dark shadows of the plum trees.

'I could kill you,' she said.

'I had to go in, we were getting nowhere.'

'You should have waited for me!' she whispered angrily. 'You always do this.'

'It wasn't planned.'

'Bullshit. Are we a partnership here, or not?'

Before Striker could respond, loud yelling noises came from within the residence. The words were impossible to make out, but the voices were definitely male and female. And Striker knew he had done his job well.

Dr Ostermann and his wife were fighting.

'What did you do in there?' Felicia asked.

He shrugged. 'I just cornered a dog.'

Felicia gave him a hard look. 'What else?'

Striker shrugged. 'I bluffed him. Told him we knew about the videos.'

'You *what*?'

'Let him think we have more than we have,' Striker said. 'It

worked, Feleesh. It connected. Like a friggin' home run. You should've seen the look on his face. He damn near had a coronary right there in the foyer.'

'But at what cost? Now he might destroy the evidence.'

Striker shook his head. 'Never. If he's making videos, then you know as well as I do what they are – his goddam trophies. He'll keep them forever, even at the expense of being caught. But he will try to hide them.'

'Probably immediately.'

'Exactly, so get ready to motor.'

Striker focused back on the house. He'd barely lifted the binoculars to his eyes when a table lamp smashed out through a front-room window. Shards of glass littered the front lawn and driveway, and the lamp came crashing down on top of Dr Ostermann's X5, denting the hood and cracking the windshield. Almost immediately, the car alarm went off and the street was filled with long, undulating wails.

'Jesus Christ,' Felicia said.

They both got up. Striker got on his phone and called Central Dispatch. Sue Rhaemer told him they were already getting a call from a frantic neighbour.

'We're already on scene,' Striker told her. 'And we're going in.'

He hung up the phone and they headed for the house.

Felicia ran beside him. They crossed the lawn, reached the roundabout, and were just nearing the front door when Striker's cell went off again. Thinking Sue Rhaemer was calling back, he snatched it up. But instead of hearing Sue's scratchy voice, he heard the hardened tone of Jim Banner.

'Noodles, I'm going into a domestic here.'

'The Ostermann house?'

'Yeah.'

'Then be careful. We got the prints back on the can of varnish. And we got a perfect hit on them.'

'Who do they come back to?'

'Who do you think?' Noodles replied. 'None other than the doctor himself. Erich Reinhold Ostermann.'

Seventy-Four

When Striker and Felicia reached the front alcove of the Ostermann mansion, they each took sides. Striker glanced at the broken shards of glass that covered the front lawn and driveway, then at the table lamp that had broken apart when smashing into the BMW. Lastly, he looked at the room above, where curtains now hung out of the window.

'Watch our backs,' he told Felicia and gestured towards the window.

'Copy. You take the door.'

Striker did. He moved up to the front door and knocked hard.

'Vancouver Police!' he yelled. 'Dr Ostermann, it's Detectives Striker and Santos – come to the door!'

No response.

He pressed the doorbell and heard the chimes go off inside the house.

'Dr Ostermann! Lexa!' he called, then added, 'Dalia? Gabriel?'

But again there was no response.

'Fuck this,' he said.

He stepped back from the door and gave it a quick once-over. The door was made from solid oak with steel hinges, and the surrounding frame looked strong. It was going to be a bitch to kick in, but what other option did they have?

Striker turned around and gave the door three heavy donkey kicks, placing the heel of his shoe between the lock and frame each time. On the third kick, the frame cracked. On the fourth, it splintered. And on the fifth, the entire structure broke apart and the front door went crashing inwards.

Striker pulled out his pistol and used the broken frame as cover. 'Chunk out,' he told Felicia. '*Chunk out!*'

She nodded and drew her pistol.

And they headed into the house.

They swept into the foyer and quickly took sides; Felicia got the east, Striker took west. Striker strained his ears to detect anything besides the blaring car alarm out front, but heard nothing.

The house was dead silent.

'It's too quiet in here,' Felicia said.

'Just be ready,' Striker told her.

Together they cleared the bottom of the house, starting with the living room and den area, then carrying on into the kitchen, a sitting room and the library.

At the far end of the hallway was the last room, the office. Striker reached it, tried the doorknob, and found it locked. He didn't so much as hesitate. He simply took a step back, then swung his leg forward and kicked the door in with one try.

The lock snapped and the door broke inwards, revealing a small secluded office. There were no windows in the room. No closets. And no other doors. Just a huge old wooden desk with a computer on it, a pair of chairs on one side, and the doctor's chair on the other.

A place for private sessions? Striker wondered. The emptiness of the room seemed odd.

'It's clear,' Felicia said.

Striker nodded. 'Upstairs then.'

They spun about and made their way back down the hall. When they reached the foyer, they turned and started up the stairs.

Felicia spoke. 'We should have a second unit for this. Patrol cops will be here soon.'

'Not soon enough,' Striker replied.

He pressed on, up the stairs.

When they reached the landing, they stepped into a hallway that led in both directions. Striker paused. A strong smell filled the hall – clean, floral, earthy. After a moment, he figured it to be herbal additives from the bath Lexa had been taking. Lavender. Or juniper, maybe.

'Hold west,' he said. 'Make sure no one comes up behind us. I'll clear the east end first.'

'Got it,' Felicia said.

Striker made his way down the hall. He came to a bathroom, complete with shower and tub, but this was not where the smell was coming from. Once cleared, he made his way down the hallway, clearing two more bedrooms along the way. The smaller one belonged to Dalia, Striker presumed, for the clothes on the chair were almost Goth in style, dark and drab, and all the same. The pictures on the wall were equally morbid. Posters of Marilyn Manson and the like.

The second bedroom was the exact opposite. A guest bedroom of sorts that looked made for a queen. The bed was immense, a king-sized, four-poster number, covered with a thick burgundy quilt that matched the colour of the drapes, which now hung out of the broken window. In the far corner of the room was a pair of high-backed floral Victorian-style chairs, and opposite them was a small bar, complete with fridge and an ice-cube machine.

Striker cleared the room then made his way down the hall,

and came up beside Felicia. She still had her pistol aimed down the other side of the landing.

'It's all clear,' he said. 'You ready?'

'Just go.'

Together, they made their way down to the west end of the hallway. They passed an old storage room, which was empty save for a few piles of boxes and an older-style television set. Then they cleared a reading room with a huge bay window that looked north over the cliffs and harbour below. Out there, the night was black and the waters below looked deep and violent.

Striker had no time for the view, and he carried on. So far they'd cleared almost two out of three floors in the house, and they had yet to run into one member of the family.

Striker didn't like it.

When they reached the only other bedroom on this floor, Striker paused. It was the master bedroom. He knew this from the way Lexa had gestured to it during their earlier conversation in the foyer.

Through the door he could smell that strong, earthy scent.

He gave Felicia the nod to make sure she was ready, then pushed open the door. Inside, a king-sized bed owned the middle of the room, unmade. Next to it, the drawers of the credenza had been opened and dumped.

'It looks like the place has been ransacked,' Felicia said.

'Or like someone was getting ready to run away in the middle of the night.'

Striker stepped into the room. He cleared the walk-in closet to his left, then made his way towards the last door, which led to an ensuite. When he reached it, Striker readied his pistol and slowly pushed the door all the way open with his foot.

What he saw inside the bathroom shocked him.

The windows were fogged, and the air was hot and humid. Along the far wall sat a Jacuzzi tub, filled to the rim with hot foamy water. The foam was not white, however, it was a deep brownish-red colour – because in the centre of the tub lay Dr Erich Ostermann.

His eyes were like a doll's eyes, wide open and unfocused, and his skin was ghostly white. One of his arms lay beneath the discoloured water of the tub; the other draped over the side. One look at it and Striker saw the meaty razor gash running down the length of the forearm, on into the wrist and palm. There were several, in fact.

Deep, grooved lines that no longer bled.

'Jesus Christ,' Felicia said. 'He killed himself.'

'Just watch our backs,' Striker said.

He stepped carefully into the room and looked around the area. On the floor, by the foot of the tub, lay an old razor knife. The blade was brownish-red.

On top of the toilet-seat lid was a note and a key.

Striker moved over to it. The paper was folded, and on the face were the two handwritten words:

Detective Striker

He gloved up and picked up the note. Opened it and read. The message was brief and direct:

Dear Detective Striker,

I have spent over fifteen years perfecting the EvenHealth programme, dedicating countless hours of my time in the selfless service of others. I have sacrificed all for the lost and the ill, and would ask you only to consider this before destroying my legacy.

Before you act too rashly – before you tell the world what I have

done — please consider this . . . intimately. The videos. They are what they are. I am not proud of them. Or of my weaknesses. To be blunt, I simply couldn't help myself. I couldn't stop, no matter how hard I tried, or how bad I felt afterwards.

Please, do not show this letter to anyone. Please do not tell the world what I have done. Especially not the other members of my profession. This is my final request.

With this letter is the key to my study.

Sincerely yours,
Doctor Erich Reinhold Ostermann

Seventy-Five

A friggin' suicide, Striker thought. He couldn't believe it was ending this way.

He read the note three more times and felt a sense of frustration wash over him. This was the coward's way out, and it left him feeling empty. Like something had been stolen from him.

It also never told him where Larisa was located.

He gently folded the paper and placed it back exactly as he had found it. Sitting beside the letter was a key to the study. Striker picked it up, then returned to the master bedroom to join Felicia.

'Suicide note?' she said.

He just nodded.

'Let's clear the rest of this damn place,' he said. 'We still need to find the rest of the family.' There was a sense of worry in his words; he could not hide it.

The quicker they got moving, the better.

They left the bedroom, then made their way down the hall to the stairway and continued up to the final floor. At the top of the stairs, the landing went three ways: east, west and one short add-on to the north.

They headed east. Down at the end was another bedroom with the door wide open. Striker and Felicia went down there. The room was very clean and orderly, with all types of clothes

hanging in the closet, and a standard-sized bed. Striker guessed the room belonged to Dr Ostermann's son, Gabriel.

From the bedroom they went back to the west side of the house. It turned into one giant loft. The room had been renovated into a movie room, complete with an overhead projector, movie-style seats with drink holders, and a surround-sound system built right into the walls. The room was impressive, and it made Striker wonder if Ostermann had watched his videos up here.

'Clear,' Felicia said.

'Clear,' Striker agreed.

He turned around and looked back into the hall. Every room had been cleared now. Every room except for one down the north hallway.

The doctor's private study.

They made their way back down the hall, then turned north along what appeared to be an add-on to the house. The hallway went on for about fifteen feet before stopping at a plain door. Striker touched the wood. It was solid oak. Strong.

Before opening it, Striker paused. He looked all around the area for wires or hidden switches. Dr Ostermann had been bat-shit crazy. No matter what he said in his letter, no matter how much he prattled on about his legacy and the welfare of his patients, Striker would never trust the man. There was nothing a madman loved more than taking a couple of cops with him.

Seeing no imminent danger, Striker turned to Felicia.

'Watch for traps.'

He reached out and grasped the doorknob. It refused to turn, so he stuck the key into the lock and gave it a twist. The lock clicked and the knob turned, and the door opened.

As it did, Striker scanned the room. What he saw surprised

him. He had expected to see another office, similar to the one downstairs. A large desk. Some reading chairs. Maybe even a file folder or two. A credenza.

He saw none of that. Instead, he saw a cabinet in the far corner of the room, composed of polished redwood and shiny brass locks. The doors to it were closed.

In the centre of the room, he saw what appeared to be a large wooden table, also made from polished redwood. It was covered with scuff marks and scratches. Opposite the table, on the wall, hung a brand-new LED widescreen with a built-in Blu-ray player.

Striker made his way into the room. When he closed in on the table, he noticed that there were heavy iron pins and hand-cuffs attached to each side. And chains. On the top right handcuff, brownish-red liquid coloured the steel. The floor below it was also stained.

'We got blood all over here,' Striker said.

Felicia looked under the table and her face tightened. 'We got torture stuff under here, too. Rods. Knives. Holy shit, a pair of pliers. Man, this guy was one sick puppy.'

Striker said nothing. He looked at the table with the bind-ings, then at the torture tools underneath it. A thought crossed his mind, and he made his way over to the redwood cabinet. Once there, he slowly opened the doors and looked inside.

Staring back at him was a black leather mask – the exact same type as the one he had seen on the suspect, back at the Mandy Gill crime scene. There were also two rows of DVDs. An exter-nal hard drive. And cameras – high-def tape, mini-disc and digital. The sight of it made his stomach tighten.

Felicia saw all this, too. 'The mother lode.'

Striker didn't reply. He was too busy taking it all in. He reached up to the top shelf and plucked up one of the Blu-ray

discs. He took it over to the wall-mounted TV, turned on the Blu-ray player, stuck in the disc and hit Play.

The TV came to life.

On the screen was a man imprisoned in a cage. He was facing away from the camera, curled up on his side. His back and legs were bleeding and he was quivering.

'Please,' he whimpered. '*Please.*'

But his voice was weak, lost.

Barely a whisper.

Behind him, half in the shadows, was a figure. Dressed in a long dark cloak. The face was hidden, but in the person's hand was a long, thin rod. Sharp steel. The end of it glistened with wetness.

'Jesus Christ,' Felicia said. 'What a sick fuck.'

Striker took another look at the DVDs in the cabinet. One of the discs had no title but it displayed today's date on the label. Thoughts of Mandy and Sarah filtered through his mind and were replaced by the image of Larisa.

It left him sick inside.

He stuck the disc in the player, but the machine couldn't read it. Swearing, he took the disc out, cleaned it off, and tried again. But the machine displayed the same message:

Unreadable format.

'*Shit.*'

'You need a computer,' Felicia said. 'There was one in Ostermann's main office.'

Striker didn't hesitate. He took the disc with him down the two flights of stairs. When they reached the main-floor foyer, Striker could hear the sound of police sirens in the faraway distance, their sad wails slicing through the night. The sound felt good to his ears, and he continued down the hall.

They made their way into Dr Ostermann's office. As Felicia

booted up the computer, Striker took note of the throw carpet on the floor. It was a small rug, less than four feet wide and eight feet long, and it sat unevenly in the room, covering more of the right side than the left.

Why would the doctor leave it that way?

Curious, he walked across the room and stepped on it. As he did, he felt a little give in the centre. Some springiness. He stepped back, grabbed hold of the corner of the rug, and pulled it across the room.

Beneath it was a hatch in the floor.

'Look at this,' he said to Felicia.

She stopped fidgeting with the computer and came up beside him. 'Wine cellar?' she asked.

'We're about to find out.'

Striker slid his fingers through the iron handle and pulled; the hatch lifted with a metallic groan and Striker let it fall to the floor on the other side. He stared down the ladder, into what looked more like a concrete bunker than an old wine cellar.

The lighting down there was dim and appeared to be fluorescent. Weak, but it did the job. As Striker stared into it, something caught his eye. Stacked on the floor, near the bottom of the ladder, were some pertinent items.

A battery pack for a cordless drill.

A box of latex gloves.

And a half-dozen packages of relay cameras.

Striker drew his pistol and gave Felicia a hard look.

'The Adder,' Felicia gasped.

'Keep your gun ready and cover me,' Striker said. 'I'm going down.'

Seventy-Six

Striker aimed his SIG Sauer and scanned the area below as he prepared to descend. There was no movement down there, just a still, murky dimness. The room appeared medium in size. Maybe twenty feet by thirty. Lots of grey concrete. A bed that was messed up. A dresser next to it with a small widescreen TV and a Blu-ray player. And a cabinet, holding a computer.

It all seemed rather ordinary.

Striker stepped on the first rung of the ladder and looked below. It was a surprising drop. Over fifteen feet down to hard concrete. He kept his gun pointed below, ready for anything unexpected, as he made his way down.

From above, Felicia covered him.

When Striker's feet touched bottom, he turned around and stared at the room before him. From this vantage point he could see that the bed was actually an old futon, and the space beneath it was empty, save for a pair of old runners.

The room smelled strongly of disinfectant. Something like bleach. And as Striker made his way around the perimeter, he found the source of the smell. Sitting in the far corner, tucked behind one of the boxes of latex gloves, was an old can of varnish.

Steinman's.

The sight made him tighten his grip on the gun.

'What you got down there?' Felicia called.

'It's a friggin' *lair*,' he called back. 'The Adder's. No doubt about it.'

'I'm coming down.'

Thoughts of getting trapped back at Sarah Rose's place flashed through Striker's mind. 'No!' he called. 'Stay up there. We need you up there covering our backs.'

'Patrol's with me.'

Striker looked up and spotted a blue uniform behind her. 'Okay, fine. But get someone to guard the top there. I don't need us getting trapped in another burning building.'

Felicia got the patrol unit to cover them, then came down the ladder and joined Striker. The moment she looked around, her claustrophobia kicked in. Striker knew it; he'd seen it in her a million times.

'You can wait upstairs,' he said. 'You don't have to be down here.'

'Just get looking.'

He did. He started with the shoes under the bed. The label inside said size ten and a half. Same as the suspect's shoe imprints they'd found back at Mandy Gill's place, in the secondary crime scene.

Striker turned the runners over and analysed the tread. Checkered. And the wear pattern on the right toe was far greater than on the left shoe, suggesting an awkward gait. Maybe from a previous knee or hip injury. Maybe something congenital. Regardless, the pattern of wear matched the sole imprints from the crime scene.

'There's no doubt,' Striker said.

'I'm getting the creeps,' Felicia said.

'Just keep your guard up. There could be traps.'

Felicia turned away and started carefully searching through the bedding on the futon; Striker left her there and approached

the cabinet. On the desktop sat a new computer case, three external back-up drives, and a mouse with keyboard. Lining the top shelf was a row of DVDs and Blu-ray discs. All of them were brand-new, unused, still covered with cellophane wrap.

Striker moved the mouse, and the monitor turned from black to blue. Across the screen was the Windows password request. A hundred different possibilities ran through Striker's head, but he opted to leave the computer untouched. One wrong attempt might be enough to lock them out or start a pre-programmed formatting application.

The Forensic guys could handle this one.

'We need Ich here,' Striker said. 'To unlock the computer and back everything up.' He pulled out his iPhone and tried to make the call, but from this deep in the bunker, surrounded by walls of concrete, he couldn't get a signal. He headed back for the ladder, put his foot on the first rung, and stopped.

To his left was a picture on the wall. A lithograph of some kind. It was a famous work. Striker couldn't recall the artist, but he knew the title.

Relativity.

It was a picture of people walking up and down different flights of stairs that defied all laws of gravity. Twisted, abnormal, unnerving.

Fitting for this place.

The print was huge, blown up, easily four feet by four feet. In a room that offered nothing else – no family photos, no posters, no knick-knacks of any kind – it seemed odd and out of place. But it was not just the picture that stole Striker's attention, it was the frame. The frame hung slightly out of kilter, the left side higher than the right.

Striker stepped towards it, pulled out his flashlight, shone it

all around the wall. On the concrete, there were faint scuff marks, ones that matched the gold-black paint of the frame.

He reached out and took hold of the painting. With one heave, he lifted it from the wall and put it down on the ground. Behind it was a strange door, half the size of a regular one. Maybe two feet wide and three feet high.

After staring at it for a half-minute, Striker realized what it was.

An old dumbwaiter.

The perfect hiding spot or escape route.

He gestured urgently for Felicia to join him. She saw what he had found and drew her pistol. She aimed it at the door and waited for Striker to open it. When he did, then aimed his flashlight inside at the gaping darkness, all they found was an empty space.

Felicia deflated and holstered her SIG; Striker leaned down and shone his flashlight up into the hole. There was a passageway there, leading up. It was large enough for a man to stand in.

Striker angled the beam towards the upper floors and saw that the dumbwaiter went all the way to the top. Right to Dr Ostermann's locked study.

Interesting.

'Why have a built-in dumbwaiter all the way down here?' Felicia said, half to herself.

'They probably used this room as an old food or wine cellar way back when,' Striker replied. 'God knows it's cool enough down here.'

He studied the dumbwaiter.

On the left side, on the inside of the post, was a pulley system. Striker grabbed the rope and slowly lowered the dumbwaiter down to his level. On the tray was a video camera, a model he had never seen before, one with an LED screen. Instead of a disc

or tape, the camera had a built-in hard drive. The camera also had a built-in motion sensor. So when Striker moved the camera, it began recording again.

He found the settings and turned off the motion sensor.

Felicia came up beside him. 'What's on it?' she asked.

'We're about to find out.'

Striker hit Play and the video began. On the screen were Dr Ostermann and Lexa, but dressed like Striker had never seen them. Dr Ostermann was naked, except for the leather collar and chain that hung around his neck; Lexa was tightly wrapped in a red leather corset, her breasts pushed up and outwards, almost falling out of the cups. Below, she wore a pair of red silk panties and stockings to match.

She tied Dr Ostermann down, face first, on the table, shackling his hands and feet to each post. Then, when he was all splayed out, she began caressing his body with a long strap of black leather.

Ostermann groaned in delight with every teasing lash. But within minutes, the lashings grew more strenuous. Fierce, even. The tail-end of the strap left huge raw red marks on the doctor's back and neck and buttocks and legs.

'Red,' he cried out. 'Red, Lexa. *RED!*'

But she acted as if she never heard their safety word and continued lashing the man. The expression on her face was one that Striker had not seen on her before – smug, controlled, *dark*.

The feed went on for another four minutes. Until Ostermann stopped moaning and groaning, and just lay there whimpering on the table like a tenderized piece of meat.

Lexa slowly approached the table, the smile on her lips stretching across her entire face. She moved slowly from corner to corner, unfastening each handcuff and setting her husband free. When they were all off, Dr Ostermann did not move. He

remained on the table, his breathing laboured and his whimpers audible.

Lexa leaned over him. Kissed him gently on his neck. Reached down and squeezed his balls.

Dr Ostermann let out a frantic cry, and Lexa smiled once more.

'You *disgust* me,' she said.

Then she dropped the leather lash across his back, stripped out of her dominatrix lingerie, and dressed once more in her green silk kimono. Without so much as a glance back, she left the room.

Dr Ostermann lay in the centre of the feed, quivering but still, with only the sounds of his whimpers and cries filling the room.

Then the video stopped.

Striker looked away from the video camera display, back at Felicia, and couldn't hide the surprise from his expression. 'The office upstairs . . . it isn't a torture room at all – the Ostermanns are into S&M sex.'

'What a couple of sick fucks,' Felicia said.

Striker thought it over, pieced it together. 'The marks we saw on Dr Ostermann's back and neck make sense now. They weren't shingles, or an injury from a fall – they were friggin' *whip* marks.'

Felicia nodded. 'It would also explain his feeble movements.'

'And why he was so embarrassed about the videos. Jesus, when I was threatening him about the murder films – he thought I was talking about his S&M videos. His home videos.'

Felicia thought it over. 'Dr Ostermann, a masochist.'

'And Lexa, a *sadist*,' Striker finished.

The word seemed wrong as he spoke it, but he couldn't help thinking that. Lexa was the one constant here. And the image of

her coming downstairs in her kimono, her skin dappled with sweat, her eyes wide and doe-like, came back to him.

'Lexa,' he said. 'Where the hell is she now?'

Felicia said nothing.

Striker placed the camera back on the dumbwaiter tray for Forensic Video to process. As he did this, thoughts of the Adder taping them returned. Striker turned from the dumbwaiter, took out his flashlight, and began going round the room, inspecting everything. There were no other cameras or microphones visible, or any other surveillance equipment, but that didn't mean none were there.

A sweep of the room would be necessary.

He shone the light under the bed and saw nothing of importance. He then shone it under the dresser and the computer cabinet. There, he stopped. On the concrete below the cabinet there were faint but visible brownish marks.

Scuff marks, just like with the painting.

'This cabinet's been moved,' he said.

He wrapped his fingers around the base of the cabinet and slowly swung it out from the wall. When he looked behind it, he saw a small hollow in the wall. About as long and high and deep as a small microwave. In it sat two rows of DVD and Blu-ray cases. Marked on all of them was the word *Back-up*, followed by different dates. Striker read through them.

One of them had been made just this morning.

He took it out and dropped it into the Blu-ray player across the room. When he turned on the TV and hit Play, the video started. What Striker saw made his blood turn cold; the video was of him and Felicia. Inside Sarah Rose's apartment. Right before the fire had started.

Felicia stepped forward. 'Jesus Christ, is that us?'

Striker said nothing. He just looked from the TV to the row

of DVD and Blu-ray discs in the nook behind the cabinet. All of them would have to be watched. Reviewed for any shred of evidence.

It would take *hours*.

He watched the feed continue until the moment when he and Felicia had managed to break out of the front door through the burning blaze. Then the video stopped—

And started once more.

The camera angle spun about, as if the camera was being picked up. And then, for one fleeting moment, the feed caught the image of a young man with wild, jet-black hair and eyes such a light green they looked transparent.

Felicia turned to look at Striker. Her face was ashen.

'The Adder isn't Dr Ostermann,' she said softly. 'It's—'

'Gabriel,' Striker said, and he could hardly believe his own word.

Gabriel Ostermann.

The boy.

The son.

And he was gone.

Seventy-Seven

The Adder walked slowly down Sasamat Trail, one of the bark-mulch pathways that snaked all through the Pacific Spirit Regional Park. When he reached the end of it, he stopped on a bluff overlooking the strait. Far below, the turbulent waters were black and deep and cold.

Like the well.

Memories of the front window of the house smashing apart after he'd thrown the lamp through it returned to him. In bits and pieces. In intermittent waves. Like a TV signal fading in and out. His actions would have attracted much attention, no doubt.

Another one of the Doctor's rules, broken.

As if sensing his thoughts, his cell phone rang and the Doctor's name flashed across the screen. The Adder looked at it for a long moment, listening to the rings, not wanting to pick it up.

One. Two. Three . . .

He finally picked up. 'I am here.'

'Have you managed to calm yourself down?'

'Yes.'

'Do you know what has happened since you left?'

'No.'

'Your father is dead, Gabriel. He committed suicide.'

The Adder said nothing.

'Come to the lake house. We will meet you there. We need to . . . *re-plan*.'

The line went dead and the Adder stood there motionlessly.

Father dead. It was a strange notion. And it made him feel somehow hollow and light. He could not understand it.

He walked to the edge of the bluff and sat down on a rotting log. As he stared out over the black waters, he took out a DVD and cradled it in his hands. This was the one. The one that had started it all. And the thought of it made his heart beat faster, made his throat turn dry.

The voices would start soon; he knew their pattern well. And so he took out his headphones and plugged them into the speaker port on his iPod. Moments later, the only file loaded, and the blissful release of the white noise began.

The Adder needed it to clear his head. To calm his nerves. And to *think*.

Clear thought was essential right now. There was no place for error. No excuse for acting hastily. He simply could not afford to. The most crucial of all moments was almost here. For Homicide Detective Jacob Striker.

That thought made the Adder smile.

The Big Surprise was coming.

He could hardly wait.

Day Three

Day Three

Seventy-Eight

It was early morning when Striker awoke from the stinging of his burned hand, and the day felt every bit a Friday. The room was dark and cold. He was in that realm, still somewhere between wake and sleep, and a sense of desperation filled him. He reached over in the darkness, felt for Felicia, and could not find her. Then he remembered she was sleeping on the couch.

That bothered him, and it woke him up fully.

He sat up in the bed, looking around the drab greyness of the room and trying to sort things out in his head. Yesterday had been a constant whirlwind, and discovering Gabriel Ostermann's room and learning he was, in fact, the Adder had sent the investigation exploding in new directions.

So much had already been done, and so much was still required. Already, he had flagged the entire family – Gabriel, Lexa and even Dalia – on all the different systems: on PRIME, CPIC, and with even Customs and Interpol. He was taking no chances with this one.

The Adder could not escape again. He was a serial killer. And serial killers never stopped killing until one of two things happened – either they were caught, or they were killed.

Striker kicked the blankets off his legs and stood up. The first thing he did was grab his iPhone from the charger and read the screen. There were no new calls, and that was disappointing.

He'd been hoping for something – for anything – from Larisa Logan.

But nothing had come in.

He dialled the number for Central Dispatch and was pleased to hear Sue Rhaemer's voice: 'CD.'

'Shouldn't you be off by now?' Striker asked.

'I already was,' she groaned. 'Got called in early. We're short. The flu's going round again.'

'Anything on the file?'

'Did I call you?' she asked.

'No.'

'Then there's your answer.'

Striker ignored her testiness and nodded as if she could see him. 'Keep me informed, Sue.'

He hung up the phone, then left his bedroom and did the usual grind. He checked on Courtney, who was still fast asleep in her bed, then put on some coffee and swallowed some Tylenol for his injured hand, then he woke Felicia. By the time they had both showered and poured a cup, it was just after six a.m. and the morning was still dark.

'You ready?' he asked her.

She offered him an eager smile. 'We're gonna find him today. I can *feel* it.'

He hoped she was right.

A half-hour later – after picking up another coffee, this time a traditional Timmy's brew – they were back at the Ostermann mansion. The sun was still asleep, the air was cold and the morning sky a deep purple smear. To Striker, it felt like they had never left the crime scene. Only now there was a patrol guard posted outside the front and back of the house. He badged the guard – some young kid he had never seen before – and went inside.

They went straight to Dr Ostermann's office. The room had already been photographed by Ident, and during the subsequent search, all sorts of files and folders of interest had been boxed as evidence.

Striker pointed to the farthest row of boxes. They were all ready-made cardboard containers, each with the case number written in thick black felt on the sides.

'You take that row,' he said to Felicia. 'I'll take the one over there.'

Felicia sipped her coffee, then made her way over.

Striker opened up the closest box and leafed through the paperwork inside. There were mounds of the stuff. Everything from paid bills to case studies to back-ups of patient files. And Striker now wished they'd brought a thermos of coffee for the day.

They were gonna need it.

As Striker went through the boxes, he made sure he kept everything in order. Nothing was more frustrating as an investigator than realizing something you'd already read was now a critical piece of evidence, but you had no idea where you'd left it. It was a lesson learned once, and learned hard, and never repeated.

The process was slow and time-consuming. By the time Striker got to the fourth box, he considered running down the road to grab them both yet another cup of coffee. He was about to suggest it when Felicia made an interested sound.

He looked over. 'What ya got?'

'Look at this,' she said.

She held up a thin white file folder. On it was a printed label with the words: Jonathon McNabb. But when she opened up the file, there were no patient reports, only a list of credit cards and bank accounts. Attached to the inside back cover was an

envelope. Felicia opened it and pulled out several pieces of identification: a BC driver's licence, a social insurance number card, even a birth certificate.

The picture on the driver's licence showed Gabriel Ostermann. 'Let me see that,' Striker said.

He took the driver's licence from Felicia and scrutinized it. Everything was done in perfect detail, from the writing on the front and back of the card to the authentic-looking hologram on the front.

'Are they fakes?' Felicia asked.

Striker raised an eyebrow. 'These are pretty good. They might be legit.'

'So then is Gabriel Ostermann's real name Jonathon McNabb, or is he using someone else's identity?'

'Call your guy at the credit bureau. Will he be in yet?'

Felicia nodded. 'They're on eastern time.'

Less than two minutes later, she hung up the phone and gave Striker the nod. 'Victim of identity theft,' she said. She pulled another file out of the same box. The name on this file was Eleanor Kingsley. When she opened up the folder, everything inside was the same as in the last folder – credit card applications, bank accounts, gas cards, and more. Attached to the back of the folder was another envelope. From it, Felicia took another stack of identification cards. Only this time the face wasn't Gabriel Ostermann's, it was Lexa's.

'Run the name with your contact,' Striker said.

She went through the process again. Two minutes later, they had another confirmed hit. Eleanor Kingsley had reported over seventy-eight thousand dollars in charges to credit cards she had never requested or received.

Striker saw the pattern.

'They're stealing everyone's identities,' he said. 'And then

taking them for every damn penny they can get from their credit. Bankrupting them.' He looked at the box Felicia was holding. It was thick with folders. Probably contained more than fifty.

'Look for Mandy Gill and Sarah Rose,' he said.

It took Felicia less than thirty seconds to find both, and when she took the IDs from the two folders, it was the same thing all over again – only this time Lexa was Sarah Rose and Dalia was Mandy Gill.

Felicia couldn't believe it. 'My God, they're a one-family crime ring.'

Striker looked at the row of boxes behind her and thought of all the file folders in each one. Eleanor Kingsley alone had been ripped off for more than seventy grand. Here they had boxes and boxes of file folders. *Hundreds* of victims.

The money count was mind-boggling.

Seventy-Nine

It was over two hours later, at quarter after nine in the morning, by the time Striker and Felicia left the Ostermann house. With them they took three cardboard boxes, jam-packed with file folders.

All possible victims of identify theft.

When they reached their vehicle, Felicia opened the trunk and Striker dropped the boxes inside. He closed the trunk, then took a moment to pull out his phone and call Courtney. She had an appointment booked with her OT this morning, and Striker wanted to make sure she attended.

The phone rang three times, then went to voicemail.

'Get up, Pumpkin,' he said. 'I'm already at work and you got an appointment with Annalisa this morning. Ten o'clock, and don't be late. I love you.'

He hung up the phone and went to put it away, but it vibrated against his hand. He looked down at the screen, expecting to see Courtney returning his call, but all he saw was a red number 1 over his phone icon.

A missed call.

He read the number and recognized it as Kirstin Dunsmuir's. Which piqued his curiosity. The woman was a pill, and colder than a popsicle enema, but no one could

question her work ethic. She had probably been at the lab all night long.

Fitting for a Death Goddess.

'That was the medical examiner who called,' he said.

Felicia made an *ugh* sound. 'I don't do Kirstin Dunsmuir before lunch.'

'She might have something.'

Felicia offered no reply, but her scowl remained.

Striker ignored it and checked his voicemail. Dunsmuir hadn't left a message, so he returned her call. She answered with her usual grace and warmth, which meant one-worded and ice cold:

'Dunsmuir.'

'It's Striker. I saw you called.'

She skipped the small talk. 'I have the results of the autopsies. There are two things of importance. Mandy Gill had a needle-mark incision. Angled medially and inferiorly, just posterior to the medial head of the clavicle.'

'Left side?' Striker asked.

'Yes.'

'What about needle marks on Sarah Rose?'

'Far too badly burned to determine. Regardless, it does appear he's injecting them.'

'But with what?'

Dunsmuir made an uncertain sound. 'I'm not entirely sure at this point – there are numerous drugs in both the victims' systems. One of them we've managed to isolate is a powerful muscle relaxant. There was enough of it in Mandy Gill's system to eventually stop her heart. We're awaiting test results for an exact determination.'

Striker thought this over. He recalled how both victims had

been facing the windows, facing into the camera. Unable to move. Unable to call for help. Barely able to breathe. He hoped they didn't realize they were going to die at that moment, but somehow he thought otherwise.

'No idea on the kind of relaxant?' he asked.

This seemed to irritate the ME and her tone dropped. 'These things take time, Detective. It's not a movie, after all.'

'I know that. Otherwise we'd have a happier ending.'

Dunsmuir let out a bemused laugh. 'There are no happy endings.'

Striker had had enough of the conversation. He told Dunsmuir to call him with the results. Then he hung up the phone.

Felicia started to get into the car. When he did not follow her lead, she stopped. 'What?' she asked.

'Is Gabriel left-handed?'

'Why?'

'Just a thought. But look at the location of the needle marks. Left side, just posterior to the clavicle. And the angle of the needle – driven in at a medial angle. If the suspect came up behind his victims, this would be a hard angle to get with the right hand.'

'And why do you think he comes up behind them?'

'No defensive wounds. Depressed or not, they would still react in some way. But here, there is nothing. It makes me think they were surprised, hence from behind.'

Felicia nodded back but said nothing, and they both piled into the car. For Striker, the phone call with Dunsmuir had been emotionally draining. And he'd had enough of the Death Goddess to last him a lifetime.

He put the car into Drive and drove. There was still tons of paperwork and police reports to comb through. Already they'd

been at it for more than three hours, and they'd barely made a dent in things. Neither one of them had gotten enough sleep the last few days, and he was feeling it.

It was going to be another long, hard day.

Eighty

The day had arrived and the sun was finally out – a piercing ball of whiteness in a sky so light it was barely blue.

Striker drove them down Main Street, then detoured on Terminal. He cut through the Starbucks drive-thru and ordered them a pair of egg-white breakfast wraps and a couple of coffees – an Americano, black, for himself, and a vanilla latte for Felicia.

Then they returned to headquarters.

Back in Homicide, the office was dead. Everywhere Striker looked, he saw empty rows of cubicles. Half the office was on their day off, the other half was out in the field, trying to write off leads and solve files. If any of them caught fire, they'd be back in before noon; otherwise, it would be an early weekend for most.

Once back at his desk, Striker set down all three boxes they had seized. There were still more boxes back at the Ostermann home, and due to the enormity of the task and their limited time, Striker had called in Clowe and Parker from Robbery to assist them. They were leafing through the files back at the Ostermann house even now.

Felicia came up beside him. She gave him an irritated look. 'We should be researching Gabriel,' she said. 'And Dalia and Lexa. We can go through all this stuff later.'

Striker shook his head. 'These folders are the reason all this

is happening. Understand the victims and you'll better understand the Adder.' Striker thought it over. They still needed to access the Police Information Retrieval System and the Law Enforcement Information Portal. 'You research Gabriel through PRIME and PIRS and LEIP; I'll keep wading through the files.'

The suggestion seemed to placate Felicia. She went to take another long sip of her latte, found it empty, then threw it in the trash can. 'I'll make us a pot,' she said, and walked across the room.

Striker was glad to have some space. He pulled over the first box and started skimming through the files.

Each was important, because of the crime that had been committed. Identity theft had ruined many a person's life, and it was the fastest growing crime in today's white-collar society. But, collectively, the files said so much more. He was less than halfway through the first box – well into the *H*s – when he saw a pattern emerging.

One that twisted up his insides.

The folder he was reading was labelled: Jeremy Heath. It was divided into sections. The first section held pages upon pages of basic information. Everything from his date of birth and mother's maiden name to computer passwords and banking information. There were also forms from the Post Office for a change of address.

The next section of the folder had every type of insurance Jeremy Heath had ever taken out, ranging from medical insurance to life insurance to disability insurance. Jeremy Heath's file even had a soldier's recompense page from Veterans' Affairs.

The third section of the folder was all the avenues of income. Visa. MasterCard. American Express. Bank names and their associated account numbers. Even pages of stocks and bonds.

The fourth and final section was composed of spreadsheets, showing lists of income from each of these cards. There was also a column for how many times each credit card limit had been upped, and if and when that request had been declined.

Everything was precise, systematic, planned.

Last of all was the envelope attached to the back of the folder that housed all the various pieces of ID. As Striker looked them over, he realized why the ID looked so real. The answer was simple.

The ID was all legitimate.

The Ostermanns hadn't been creating fake IDs, they had been obtaining real identification from the original source. All the driver licences, social insurance number cards and birth certificates were legitimate issue. He had never seen anything like it, not on this scale.

He showed all this to Felicia. 'They've actually attended the motor vehicle branch and have had their own pictures implemented.'

'They're friggin' experts,' she said.

He nodded solemnly. 'And they're systematically destroying people's lives. Even worse, they're going after all the marginal-ized victims.' His own words triggered some darker thoughts, and he got on the phone with the Collins Group.

The Collins Group was a private company, run by ex-cop Tom Collins – a friend of Striker's from years past. Collins had worked primarily in Financial Crime during his twenty-year stint with the VPD, and he had carried that expertise with him into his new endeavours of investigating corporate insurance fraud. When Striker told the receptionist who he was, she trans-ferred him without question.

'Tom Collins,' Striker said. 'How's my favourite highball?'

The man on the other end of the phone let out a gruff laugh.

'Shipwreck. Good to hear from you, man. I hear you had some problems last year over at St Patrick's.'

That made Striker pause. 'Yeah, memories better left forgotten,' he finally said. 'Look, I got some victims of identity theft here, and I was wondering if you could research them a bit for me.'

'How fast you need it?'

'Like yesterday.'

'I should have let it ring to voicemail.'

Striker just laughed and gave the man a list of the names he had accumulated from the boxes.

'And what exactly are we looking for?' Collins asked.

'You'll know it when you find it,' Striker said. 'I need this done fast. Today sometime.'

Collins let out a sour laugh. 'Your way or the highway, like always, huh?'

'What can I say? I'm particular.'

He hung up the phone, feeling better. He liked Tom. The man had been a good cop and a better friend. It had been too long since they'd seen one another.

Typical in the world of policing.

He looked back at Felicia, who had her head buried in the computer. 'What are you finding on Gabriel in PRIME?'

She looked up as if she was only now aware that his conversation with Collins had ended, and turned the screen to face him. 'With the exception of Dr Ostermann, there's not a whole lot on any of them,' she said. 'Gabriel is carded in a few of the police reports as a witness, but that was only due to car accidents. There's also a report here from almost twelve years ago. He must've been, what, eight at the time.'

'What does it say?'

'I can't bring it up, it's privatized, and it's a Burnaby file.'

'We still need it,' he said.

'Well, *duh*!' She laughed at the surprised look on his face. 'I've already left a message for the detective in charge. Get this: her last name is *Constable*. Can you believe that? Detective Constable.'

Striker grinned. 'Well, if she ever makes *Chief* Constable, the papers will have a field day with it.'

'Yeah, no kidding. I'm just waiting for her to get back to me.'

'What about Lexa?' he asked.

'In PRIME? Lexa is listed only once. Under a fingerprint file.'

'Probably for when she got her criminal record check done for nursing.'

'Bang on,' Felicia said. 'As for Dalia, she is a complete non-entity. Not in any of the systems. She doesn't exist.'

Striker thought this over.

'Run both their vehicles for tickets. Any infraction. Speeding. Red light. Parking. I don't care. Just run it all.'

Felicia didn't move. 'We already know Ostermann drove like a maniac.'

'I'm not interested in the offence, I'm interested in the locations.'

Felicia said nothing and turned back to the computer. After a few clicks, she made an interested sound. 'Hey, look at this. We know the X5 has streams of tickets, but the Land Rover, which is registered to Lexa, has only three tickets – all of them on the Trans-Canada Highway.'

This piqued Striker's interest. 'Where exactly?'

'One out near Furry Creek, and the other two just outside of Whistler Village.' She looked up. 'Maybe they have a cabin there, or something. I'll check it out.' She turned around and got on the phone to Whistler's registrar office; while she talked, Striker continued going through the boxes of files. When he

finished the *K*s and started the *L*s, he found one file that made him pause.

Logan, Larisa.

'Holy shit,' he said.

He opened up the file, but it was empty.

Confused, he looked back in the box for any loose papers, but found none. The words on the tab stared back at him. Made him angry. He searched the next three files to see if Larisa's paperwork had accidentally slipped into the wrong folder.

None had.

He sat there, letting everything sink in and feeling sick about it. He picked up his desk phone and checked his voice messages. There were seven, but none from Larisa, and none relevant to the file.

No time for them now.

He archived the phone messages and looked through his emails. Again, there were tons of messages, but nothing pertinent to this investigation. Irritated, he brought up the email Larisa had sent him the previous day and made another reply to it:

To. L.Logan@gmail.com
Subject: Contact me!

Larisa,
Please tell me where you are! Or go to the nearest police station and call me. Dr Ostermann is *dead*. Gabriel and Lexa and Dalia are missing. They are very dangerous. Beware of them. Come in or call me. Please!
– Jacob

He looked at the message for a moment, hoping it was personal enough to make her respond. He hit Enter and the message sent. After that, he sat there for a long moment, waiting for a response.

None came. And after recalling the way things had gone down at the Arabic Beans coffee shop at Metrotown, Striker wondered if one ever would.

It was doubtful.

The woman no longer trusted him. She trusted no one. She was all alone and in hiding. And the longer she stayed missing, the worse their chances of finding her became. It was a cold, hard fact. But it was real.

They were running out of time.

Eighty-One

It was morning by the time the Adder reached his destination. He was tired. He had not slept all night. He was hungry. He was cold.

He rounded the cabin from the north in the mid-morning light, and stood on the back deck. As he breathed out, the warmth and moisture from his breath fogged the air. He stared out over the lake. The edges were still covered with a fine layer of ice, and the weeds and reeds were frozen in place. The air smelled strongly of pine and cedar. Morning sun broke the top of the mountains to the far east. It gleamed on the cold, calm waters of the lake.

It was the perfect day. The kind of morning every skier and snowboarder craved all season long. Crisp, clear, cold. It should have been beautiful.

But the Adder could focus on none of this. All he saw was one bad memory. And the images in his head. Ones that had once been terrifying but now seemed like faded stills from a different life. A different world.

And in some sense, that was exactly what they were.

The sliding glass door opened behind him with a soft rolling sound.

'Gabriel,' a feminine voice said. Soft, and with emotion. With *relief*. And the Adder immediately knew it to be Dalia. She was

the only one who cared. The only one who had *ever* cared. She came up behind him and wrapped her arms around his chest, then let loose a gasp and shivered. 'You're so cold,' she said softly. 'Come inside. Later on, I'll help you warm up.'

He said nothing; he merely turned around and walked with her towards the cabin. Before entering, he stopped.

Thought.

He knelt down and removed the DVD from his pocket. It was Disc 1, the only copy he had left, and the only one that truly mattered. He slid it beneath the porch steps, far into the back where it was out of view. Then he stood up and moved into the warmth of the cabin. He'd barely stepped foot on the ceramic tile when the smell of green tea hit him. And then the Doctor came storming into the kitchen. Her eyes were set and dark, her face so tight it looked bloodless.

'It's about time – you fool,' she said.

Dalia stepped forward. 'Mother, please—'

'To your room, girl.'

'But Mother—'

'To your room!'

Lexa Ostermann stepped forward and gave the Girl a back-handed strike – a sharp, hard *SLAP!* that resonated like the crack of a whip. Dalia recoiled from the blow and grabbed her cheek. Sobbing, she spun from the kitchen and raced up the stairs to the second floor of the cabin.

The Adder watched her go, but did nothing. A strange tingling sensation was tickling the back of his mind. His heart. His entire body.

And he did not like it.

'You're a fool,' the Doctor continued. 'Everything, ruined. Years of work, ruined. Our family, ruined!'

'I did nothing.'

'Your *videos*,' she said, and there was ice in her words. 'They are what set everything off. Your father, dead. The police, hunting us down. Like animals, Gabriel. Like animals!'

He said nothing, and his silence only seemed to infuriate her more.

'Outside. Now.'

He looked out of the sliding glass door. 'There is no reason.'

'You know the rules.'

'But there is no well here,' he started, then he saw the lake.

'Outside,' the Doctor ordered. 'I will not tell you again.'

The Adder said nothing for a long moment, then he nodded absently and walked back out through the door. The moment he left the kitchen, the cold wind slapped his face. Sharp, stinging, burning his skin and eyes. He marched across the slippery wooden porch, down the steps and across the small back yard. The frozen blades of grass crunched beneath his feet. Then he was at the edge of the lake. Memories of the past *deluged* him. Memories of William.

He could not bear it.

'Take off your clothes,' the Doctor ordered.

Mechanically, the Adder did as instructed, folding them neatly and placing the articles one on top of the other. Shoes, then pants, then shirt. When he was completely naked – when the winter wind was cutting into him like an icy blade – the Doctor stepped closer.

'Into the lake.'

Without so much as a word, the Adder stepped forward until the soles of his feet touched the thin ice of the lake. The ice cracked, and broke beneath his weight, and the sounds of laughter grew in his ears and the image of William was suddenly there before his eyes. A little boy running and giggling on the lake.

He stopped moving.

'Into the lake,' the Doctor said again.

But this time, the Adder did not respond.

'I *order* you into the lake.'

The Adder turned. Faced her.

'No,' he said. 'I will not do this any more.' And for the first time in his memory – the first time since William's death – the Adder felt more than alive, he felt *awake*.

The Doctor's face took on a shocked look, and then she nodded slowly. 'I always knew this day would come, Gabriel. Very well then. You have finally left the past behind you. Pick up your clothes and join me in the cabin. We have much to discuss.'

The Adder nodded. He bent over to pick up his clothes and suddenly sensed movement beside him. He turned – but was far too slow. A sharp pricking sensation stung his neck, and he knew the needle had gone in.

He jerked backwards, stunned, and felt a strange hot warmth rush from his neck down his arms. The flow carried on through his body, down his legs, and even up into the top of his head – a strange numb warmth. Almost immediately, his muscles grew weak and he felt himself folding inwards. His legs trembled, then gave out, and he collapsed on the edge of the lake.

A strange, distorted sound filled the air, and the Adder realized it was the Doctor. She was laughing at him. One second there was only white sun and blue sky above him; the next moment, the Doctor was there, looking down at him with a dark smile on her lips.

'Mivacurium chloride,' she said. 'How does it feel to be on the receiving end, for a change?'

The Adder could not speak. He looked up at her melting face and tried to respond, tried to say something – what, he had no idea – but his lips would not move.

'There is a certain set order, Gabriel,' the Doctor continued. 'A *hierarchy*. And you need to remember your place within it.'

The mask she wore crumbled away in pieces, and the Adder saw her for everything that she was. Everything she had always been.

The monster beneath.

He felt her grab his legs. Felt his body being dragged along the ground. There was a wet, cold feeling surrounding his legs and hips, and he knew she had left him in the lake. Cold. So terribly cold. And the sky was black and growing blacker by the second. After a while, the sky faded. And eventually the sun burned out, leaving him with nothing but black.

Eighty-Two

Felicia hung up the phone. 'Nothing comes back,' she said.

Striker cursed. 'Nothing?'

'*Zilch*. The only address the registrar's office has on file is their house on Belmont.'

Striker thought this over. 'What about using EvenHealth as an entity?' he asked.

'Already one step ahead of you. EvenHealth as an entity comes back to every clinic the programme is associated with — and there's more than two dozen all across the city. Not to mention the rest of the Lower Mainland. How many clinics there are out there in total, I have no idea.'

Striker frowned. It left them with nothing. All they had was a house where Lexa and her children had fled from, and a pair of speeding tickets from the Whistler Village area.

He met Felicia's stare. 'If you were Lexa Ostermann and you needed somewhere to store some extra cash and ID, where would you go?'

'A PO box.'

'Agreed. But a post office box is only accessible during business hours. Normal people like you and me could always wait till the next business day, but someone involved in a scam like this would have to run at a moment's notice. So where else would you go?'

Felicia was quiet for a moment, then shook her head. 'There's only one other place I can think of – where she works. The clinic her husband owns.'

'Exactly,' he said. 'It's time to go to Mapleview.'

At exactly ten-thirty, Striker parked the undercover cruiser by the roundabout and stepped out. With the morning sun now rising high overhead, and backed by brilliant blue sky, the modern clinic of Mapleview looked pleasant enough. But all Striker could think of was when they'd come there to kidnap Dr Ostermann and intercept Billy Mercury. That had happened at three o'clock yesterday afternoon.

It felt like a lifetime ago.

'I'm starting to hate this place,' he said.

'You're preaching to the choir,' Felicia replied. She started up the old cement stairs, and Striker went with her. The moment they walked through the wired-glass double doors into the ante-chamber of the facility, the receptionist behind the desk looked up. Her face took on a pleasant look, and she smiled at them.

'Detectives,' she said. 'Good morning.'

Striker smiled. Obviously she hadn't heard the news of Dr Ostermann's demise and the family's disappearance.

'Good morning back,' he said. He approached the front desk, smiled at the woman, reached out and gently touched her hand. 'You know, in all the pandemonium yesterday, I never did get your name.'

She smiled at his concern. 'It's Pam,' she said. 'Well, *Pamela*. Pamela O'Malley.'

'I'm actually surprised to see you in here today.'

She looked around and shrugged. 'Everyone else called in sick, and someone has to be here for the patients.'

'It's very decent of you.'

'Yeah, good job,' Felicia added.

Striker met the woman's stare. 'How are *you* coping, Pam? If you need a card for Victim Services, I can give you one.' He looked around the room as if suddenly realizing where he was, and grinned. 'Actually, if you need some therapy, I guess you're probably covered.'

When the receptionist smiled and chuckled at his comment, Striker got down to business.

'I need to speak with one of your staff members,' he began.

'Dr Ostermann still isn't in yet.'

'Actually, I was looking for *Lexa*.'

The smile on the woman's face fell away. 'Mrs Ostermann isn't in yet either. She doesn't normally work till the afternoon.'

'You almost say that with relief,' Striker said. When the woman didn't know how to respond, he smiled at her and lowered his voice. 'It's okay. I've dealt with her only twice – and that's been enough for me. But duty calls, you know.'

The receptionist laughed softly. 'Yes, Mrs Ostermann can be a bit . . . *demanding* at times.'

'She's a pill,' Felicia said boldly.

The receptionist laughed again.

'So she hasn't been in here today?' Striker clarified.

'No. She shouldn't be in until one o'clock. And you can pretty much set your watch by it. Mrs Ostermann is always extremely punctual and orderly with everything she does. Even the group sessions. God forbid one of them comes in even a minute late. She kicks them out and sends them home.'

Felicia asked, 'Which group is that?'

'Oh, all the groups. But especially the SILC classes – are you familiar with the programme?'

'Yes, we are,' Striker said. 'Does she confer with Dr Ostermann

before sending his patients home? These are, after all, his sessions, right?'

'Yes, they are. But Mrs Ostermann does fill in.'

Striker found this interesting. 'Fill in? A *nurse* holds the session in place of a qualified psychiatrist?'

For a moment, the receptionist's face tightened, as if she was worried she had said too much. 'Maybe I shouldn't—'

'Hey, it's okay,' Striker told her. 'I'm not going to press Mrs Ostermann on anything. You got my word on that. I just find it surprising.'

'It's not without its merit,' the woman replied. 'Mrs Ostermann does have extra training.'

'What kind of extra training?' Felicia asked.

'I don't really know, for sure. But she took much of her training in Europe, and she's not one to talk about it. Not one to talk about anything, really. Especially not with staff.'

'Where in Europe?' Striker pressed.

'The Czech Republic.'

He nodded. 'How would you know that when she never talks about it?'

'Dr Ostermann did once. A long time ago. Over a year maybe.'

Striker rested his arm on the front counter and tried to look casual. 'Really? And you remember it.'

The woman's face took on a distant look. 'It's kind of hard to forget. Dr Ostermann was talking to Dr Richter about what courses were considered *transferable* from overseas. During the conversation, he mentioned that Mrs Ostermann had grown up in the Czech Republic and had had problems transferring her university credits.'

'Which university?'

'Charles, I think. I'm not sure exactly where it is.'

'It's in Prague,' Striker said. 'Charles Bridge.'

'And what next?' Felicia asked.

The woman's cheeks reddened further. 'Next? Oh, Mrs Oster-mann got angry. *Very* angry. I'd never seen her so . . . enraged – she is a very private person, you know.'

Striker nodded at this.

Private, he thought. And full of secrets.

He took out a business card and wrote down his cell number on the back. When he handed it to the receptionist, he made sure they had eye contact. 'If Lexa or her children return here, I need you to leave the building right away. Do you understand me, Pam?'

The woman looked confused. 'Leave the building?'

'Immediately,' he stressed. 'Make an excuse. Leave to check on one of the patients. And then, the first chance you have, I want you to leave the building and call my cell. Right away. Do you understand?'

The woman nodded slowly.

'And if Dr Ostermann comes in?'

Striker smiled wryly.

'Then I don't think my number's gonna help.'

Eighty-Three

After fully debriefing the receptionist on what had happened with Dr Ostermann's suicide and the subsequent disappearance of his family, Striker and Felicia asked to see Lexa's office.

The receptionist, still looking rattled, nodded daftly. She opened her desk drawer and pulled out a key. 'She locks it,' she said, and led them down the hall. When they rounded the east corner, they came across one room with a dark red door. 'This is Mrs Ostermann's office. She wanted it on the east side of the facility; all the other doctors are on the west.'

'I didn't realize the facility was so big,' Felicia said.

'It's actually not,' the receptionist said. 'It's just a strange layout.' She unlocked the door for them. Before moving out of the way, she fixed Striker with a hard stare. 'Please . . . if you're going to take anything, let me know. I should at least keep a record of things.'

'Of course, Pam,' Striker said. 'Have you ever been in there before?'

She shook her head. 'No one has. Like I said before, Mrs Ostermann is a very private person. She doesn't even allow the other doctors inside. It is always under lock and key, and to be honest, I think she would fire me on the spot if she ever saw me in there – no matter the reason.'

Striker nodded. He said goodbye to Pam, then went inside

the office with Felicia and closed the door behind them. As he turned around, he scanned the room.

It was very drab, and surprisingly, very sparse. Just a black walnut wood desk, a burgundy leather chair, and a computer terminal. No plants or flowers decorated the shelves. No pictures or diplomas adorned the walls. There weren't even any photographs of her family.

Felicia saw the oddness of it too. 'Talk about taking minimalism to the extreme.'

Striker walked over to the desk and opened both drawers. Not much was inside them, except for basic office supplies and a short row of file folders. Striker went through them all, carefully reading each one. All of them contained numerous patient files, but none of the names stood out to him. He took down the names so they could run them through the system later.

Then he looked at the computer. The screen was black, but when he moved the mouse the screensaver vanished. No password. No logon. Just right to the desktop. Striker started browsing through the system. He found nothing, not even one file.

'A new computer,' he said.

'Or a fresh install,' Felicia added.

He looked around for an external backup drive, but found none. He then scanned the office shelves. They were filled with medical and psychological textbooks. They all looked brand new. Like they had never been touched.

He opened one – *The Diagnostics and Statistics Manual* – and felt the inflexible give of the book's spine. None of the pages had been marked up, and no hidden papers were tucked inside the book.

He went through all the books, flipping the pages of each one and finding nothing inside. When done, Striker put the last

book back, and paused. At the end of the shelf sat a lone file folder. Red in colour. He picked it up. On the tab were the words: *Medical Billing Codes*. He opened it up, saw the list of codes, and showed it to Felicia:

10-14141ML-MG900412,
09-29292TIG-SR730128,

and more. The list was several pages long.

'Strange,' he noted. 'If these are Medical Service Plan codes, why not just print them out from the government website? Why go to all the bother of writing them down yourself?'

Felicia looked them over. 'And what do they mean, for that matter? Look at them, they're all in a different format.'

Striker was confused. 'I don't follow you.'

'Most computer programs use similar codes,' she explained. 'Look at PRIME, for example. Everything there is separated by four-digit codes: 2117 is a Suspicious Circumstance. 2118 is a Suspicious Person. 2119 is a Suspicious Vehicle. They are all listed in a pattern. But not these numbers. They're all over the map – as if they're from more than one system.'

Striker looked back at the numbers, and saw she was right. They took the file folder with them, left the office, and stopped at the receptionist's desk on the way out. Pam was still sitting there, looking lost and out of place.

Striker approached her. 'Do you have a book on Medical Service Plan codes?'

Pam blinked as if coming out of a dream. 'Medical Service Plan? Well, no. No, we don't. We would never have use of it.'

'Why not? How do you bill?'

'Because everything here is private. All the medical goes through Riverglen.'

Striker frowned at that; they would have to look the codes up later. He started to leave, then stopped.

'Are you familiar with MSP codes?' he asked.

The receptionist nodded. 'At the other clinic, I do all the billing – and they're completely covered by medical.'

Striker open the folder. He showed the list to Pam. 'Are these Medical Service Plan codes?' he asked.

The receptionist looked at the list for less than a few seconds. 'Not that I recognize.'

Striker closed the file.

'Thanks,' he said. 'I didn't think so.'

Eighty-Four

Striker and Felicia pulled out of the Mapleview parking lot and headed north on Boundary Road. He drove right to the lane behind the Esso gas station on Hastings Street. It housed an On the Run coffee shop, and was a common place where Patrol grabbed coffee after their morning briefings.

'More caffeine?' Felicia asked.

Striker nodded. 'I need one. It helps me think.'

They exited the vehicle, grabbed a couple of coffees, and returned to the lane. They stood outside the car, drinking in the frosty air because Striker liked it that way. The cold always invigorated him.

'Everything we know so far about Lexa Ostermann has been a lie,' he said. 'From the way she presented herself as the frightened victim at her home, to the role she's been playing at the clinic.'

Felicia sipped her coffee. 'Hey, give the psycho credit. She was good at it. She definitely made it look like Ostermann was the one in control of their household, and it was the exact opposite.' She shook her head. 'My God, when I think of her lashing that poor man and him screaming out, "Red. Red! *Red!*" it turns my stomach.'

'Personally, I would have picked *stop* for a safety word. Creates less confusion.'

Felicia laughed, and Striker continued.

'The point is we thought we knew the woman, and she had the wool pulled over our eyes. It makes me wonder what else we don't know about her that we think we do. The vital stuff.'

'Like her name,' Felicia said.

'Exactly. Name, date of birth, place of birth – all those details.'

Felicia took out her phone. 'I got a contact in Victoria,' she said. 'I'll look into her maiden names.'

Striker was glad to hear it. Victoria was the central location for the Vital Statistics Agency, the place where legal name changes and marriage records were kept for all of British Columbia.

'Check the marriage records, too,' he suggested.

She gave him one of her *I'm not an idiot* stares and waited for the call to be answered.

Striker let her be. Dealing with any form of the Canadian government, be it Stats Canada, Canada Revenue, or the Vital Statistics Agency, was always an exercise in frustration. Furthermore, he needed Felicia to do it, because he didn't have any contacts there. To make use of his time while he waited, he called Central Dispatch once more to see if there had been any hits on the Ostermann family.

Sue gave him her trademark response. 'Have I called you?'

'No.'

'Then there's your answer.'

Sue Rhaemer was more on top of things than a cherry on a sundae, and she had never let him down once. He could tell by her tone she was irritated he was even questioning her.

'Thanks, Sue,' he said. 'I'm just desperate here, is all.'

'You owe me a Coke.'

'Over ice,' he said.

He hung up the phone and looked at Felicia. She was still

dealing with her contact at the Vital Statistics Agency, and the look on her face was one of tentative hope. When she began writing information down in her notebook, Striker felt a glimmer of optimism. She hung up and smiled at him.

'Well?' he asked.

'Anytime you need info, you just come to momma, darling.'

Striker laughed. 'I've heard that before. Come on, Feleesh.'

'Fine, fine. But get this: Lexa married Dr Ostermann exactly ten years ago this month.'

'*Ten* years ago?' Striker asked. He thought it over. 'That would mean that Gabriel was only eight when they got married, and Dalia was five. So the kids were either born out of wedlock, or—'

'They're not siblings,' Felicia finished. 'At least not by blood. I verified it through Vital Stats. Gabriel was born a lone child to Wilma and Erich Ostermann eighteen years ago. Wilma died of cancer six years later, and barely two years after that, Erich remarried to Lexa.'

'What was Lexa's maiden name at the time?'

'Smith.'

Striker found that unsurprising. After Lee, Smith was the most common surname in all of North America – definitely the most common among Caucasians. It made searching information on her more of a hassle, and he doubted the validity of the name anyway.

'Is the name legit?' he asked.

Felicia shook her head. 'Phoney as a three-dollar bill. If you go farther back into the name records, she was originally named Jarvis from a previous marriage that lasted only three years – but that marriage took place fifteen years ago.'

'Which would match Dalia's age.'

Felicia nodded. 'Exactly. Lexa has had a list of names over the

years. And it doesn't stop there. She had requested a previous name change even before that – when she first came to Canada by way of Toronto. Her immigrant name was Novak.'

'Novak?' Striker said. He thought of the name for a brief moment, then brought out his iPhone. 'I don't know a whole lot of Czech names, but I do recognize Novak.' He punched the name into the Google search engine, then nodded when he saw the result. 'Big surprise. Smith is the most popular name in Canada, Novak is the most common name in the Czech Republic. Where did she emigrate from?'

'Berlin,' Felicia said.

'Yet the receptionist back at Mapleview said Lexa was from Prague.'

'And Lexa was none-too-happy about her knowing.'

Striker Googled Charles University, and got the number. He looked at his watch and saw it was slowly approaching noon in Vancouver. It would be around 8 p.m. there.

He called up the Information and Advisory section of Charles University and was relieved to find a person who was fluent in English. Less than ten minutes later, he got off the phone and gave Felicia a hard stare.

'She went there all right, under the name Novak – and for *eight* years.'

'Why so long? Did she change her programme?'

Striker offered a grave stare. 'She didn't go there for a nursing degree, she's a friggin' doctor. She minored in *psychology*.'

Felicia's face took on a stunned look, but then she nodded. 'It actually makes sense, when you put it all together. Lexa gets her medical degree over there, and comes to Canada.'

'But not all her courses are transferable,' Striker pointed out.

'So she finds a man who's also a forensic psychiatrist.'

'Erich Ostermann. Who just happens to own his own clinic.'

'Where she'll have access to all the patients she wants.'

'Not patients,' Striker said. '*Victims.*'

Felicia thought this over for a long moment, then shook her head. 'There's one small problem here. Why not just take the extra courses required to make her degree recognized over here? I mean, think of it, she put in eight years towards it. Why down-grade to nursing after all that?'

'I can think of two reasons,' Striker said. 'One, it's easier to hide in the background when the police come knocking – every-one thinks of the doctor, not the nurse.'

'And two?'

'Because she couldn't. Lexa Novak was already on the run.'

Eighty-Five

It was a blur, really. A muddled white haze that slowly pushed away the darkness. And William was there, calling for him to *Get up, Gabriel! Get up! You must get up!* And then William was shaking him. Shaking him fiercely. Shaking him so hard his entire body shook like a child's rag doll.

'Get up, Gabriel.'

And the clouds slowly thinned.

'Get up!'

Slowly lifted.

'GABRIEL!'

And he could see blue sky once more.

The Adder lifted his head off the cold, hard earth and it felt like it weighed a million pounds. As he awoke, so did the pain – a cold sharp stabbing sensation. Like a trillion needles poking the skin all over his body, from his head to his feet.

But his legs, they were the worst.

Sharp, *biting* pain, and yet they were also numb. Strangely, achingly numb.

It made no sense.

With all the strength he could muster, the Adder sat up and looked at his legs. They were half submerged in the icy waters of the lake, and they were whiter than the ice.

'Get up, Gabriel!' he heard from behind him.

Whispers.

Desperate panicked whispers.

And he knew that it was Dalia. Somewhere behind him. Up above. Her bedroom window perhaps.

He was too weak to turn around and look.

'Gabriel, you must get inside!'

Without thought, without real intention, the Adder tried to bend his knees. Tried to remove his legs from the icy cold waters of the lake. But his muscles refused to obey the commands of his mind. They were like dead chunks of flesh attached to his body. Useless pieces of meat.

He rolled over, on to his belly, and felt the cold sharpness of the rocks against his skin. To his left, less than an arm's reach away, were his clothes. But he could not reach for them. His mind was slowly clearing now. Ever so slowly. And his rationale was coming back in blips.

The cabin . . .

The cabin was the only chance for survival.

And so inch by inch, arm pull by arm pull, the Adder dragged his body from the lake. Dragged himself up the gravelly beach. Across the frozen lawn. Even up the slippery wood of the porch steps. The back door was still wide open, and he wondered why.

A test from the Doctor? A goal?

Or one of her many taunts?

In the end, it did not matter. He pulled himself inside, his useless legs dragging behind him. When he reached the kitchen, he saw the Doctor.

She was seated at the table, a steaming cup in one hand, her newspaper in the other. She sipped her drink, placed the cup carefully back on the saucer, and then looked down to face him. 'Welcome home, Gabriel,' she said. 'I trust you have learned yet another lesson today.'

He said nothing back. He could not. And after a moment, the Doctor stood and walked away. Out of the front door of the cabin.

As he lay there, waking, returning to life, the heat from the furnace vents blasted on his torso and legs. His skin went from that strange numbness to a cold piercing fire. He ground his teeth and wanted to scream. Wanted to wail with every ounce of strength his lungs had left.

But the Adder did not.

Instead, he lay there, his mind number than his body, and he thought of the only thing left in this world that brought him any true pleasure. The final doorway. The moment of release. The only exit from this world.

The Beautiful Escape.

It was coming once more, and this time for Jacob Striker. The thought almost made the Adder smile.

It was going to be a truly wonderful moment.

Eighty-Six

Striker wanted to run Lexa Ostermann and all her aliases through Interpol – the International Criminal Police Organization. Interpol's primary purpose was to facilitate cooperation between police departments from almost two hundred countries. Essentially, it was a spider's web of information. Starting there was their best bet.

They headed back for Homicide.

When they got there, Striker was surprised to find the office busy, and upon speaking to fellow detective Jana Aiken, learned that there'd been another gang shooting on the Granville Strip.

Nothing interesting.

He found his way to his cubicle and sat down. The computer was still running, but locked, so he logged on and quickly checked his email. No message from Larisa. No voicemail either. Frustrated, he initiated Versadex and loaded the Query page for Interpol.

As far as Striker knew, Lexa had no criminal record, not that it mattered. The database listed everything from wanted criminals to missing children to stolen property. Striker was hoping Lexa would be there, in some form or another; how, he didn't much care. All he wanted was a lead.

Instead of starting with Ostermann, Striker typed in the oldest name they knew of:

Lexa Novak.

For a date of birth, he typed in an age range of thirty-five to forty-eight.

The query came back within thirty seconds to a positive hit, low score, meaning that the details provided matched perfectly but the details provided were few and vague. There were over thirty hits.

Striker sorted through them all until he found one that matched:

Lexa Novak. Forty-six years of age.
167 cm. 59 kgs. Caucasian.
Hair: blonde. Eyes: blue. Build: medium.
Place of birth: Mesto Roztoky, České Republiky.

Striker looked up the name of the town and saw that it was not far from Prague. He looked for any tattoo or scar descriptions, but found none. He scrolled down the page and came to a Remarks section.

What he saw made him smile.

Policie České Republiky
Person of Interest. Identity Fraud.
Contact Detective Lundtiz. 974 852 319.

'*České?*' Felicia asked.

Striker nodded. 'Police of the Czech Republic,' he explained. 'We got a legitimate possible.'

He picked up the landline and dialled. The number took a long time to connect, but then it started to ring. The man who answered spoke in limited English, but managed to convey to Striker that Detective Lundtiz was now *Inspector* Lundtiz,

working in the Unit for Combating Corruption and Financial Crime.

He patched Striker through.

After another set of rings, Striker's call was answered by a receptionist and, after again explaining who he was and why he was calling, he was transferred to the main line.

As Striker waited for the inspector, Felicia got the call from one of the cops she knew in Burnaby South. The privatized file from Gabriel's childhood was ready. She gave Striker the thumbs up, then left to pick it up from the Burnaby North detachment.

Striker waved goodbye and waited on hold.

After a long pause, the phone was picked up. 'Good evening, Detective Striker, this is Inspector Lundtiz.'

Striker was surprised to hear that the inspector spoke with good English and had almost no accent. 'Good evening, Inspector. Thanks for taking my call. I'm enquiring about—'

'Lexa Kaleena Novak,' Lundtiz replied. 'Yes, I know her quite well. *Intimately* well, I would say. I spent many months following this woman before she disappeared on me. That was many years ago. Almost twenty, I would think. My God . . .'

'Well, she's been found in Vancouver, Canada,' Striker said.

'Has she killed again?'

The words shocked Striker. 'Has she killed there?'

'Undoubtedly. Proving that, however, was another matter.'

Striker said nothing for a moment, then took out his notebook and a pen. 'What exactly do you know about this woman?'

'A great deal.'

'I've got the time.'

The inspector cleared his throat and began speaking. 'I have the file right in front of me, though I went over it so many times, I practically know it all by memory. Lexa Novak was born in the

city of Prague. I'm sure you've heard of it, Charles Bridge and all.'

'I'm aware of it.'

'She grew up one of three sisters. Katerna was eldest, followed by Nava, and then Lexa. The family was upper class. Very well known. Her father, Dagan, was a well-respected man in these parts – a doctor with his hand in politics.'

'Sounds powerful,' Striker noted.

'He was. I remember him. And with Lena for a wife, every man around the town envied him. Lena was beautiful, Lena was the perfect wife and mother, and Lena brought with her a family fortune.'

'*Elite* upper class,' Striker said.

'Entirely. And from an outsider's perspective, they were living the dream. But home life was very different. Dagan Novak was a *sadist*. He took great pleasure in dominating his family, abusing them in all ways – psychologically, physically, even sexually, once the girls reached a certain age. Life in the Novak family was an existence of helplessness and torture. I am ashamed to say the police of this time failed the family utterly.'

'They knew?'

'It was reported. But because of Dagan's social and political connections, the matter was – how do you say it? – *conveniently overlooked.*'

Striker frowned. It was a situation he had seen before as well. 'What happened to the rest of the family?'

'Lena, the mother, supposedly left the family and relocated to Paris, where she had other family connections. Yet when I tried to locate her, the search quickly reached a dead end. I have no doubt that Dagan murdered her.'

'And the other girls?'

'The story is quite sad, I'm afraid. Even beyond the abuse.'

Striker shook his head. 'I don't follow.'

'The eldest of the sisters, Katerna, had to be hospitalized when she was but sixteen years of age. For severe schizophrenia. Three years after that, Nava was also afflicted with the illness.'

'A genetic link.' Striker thought this over. Given the history, it was unsurprising that Lexa had turned to a career of psychiatry. 'Lexa must have lived in constant fear of acquiring this illness.'

'The illness haunted her, tortured her . . . And I think it was the turning point of her freedom. The so-called fuse that set her off. It was not long after the middle child was hospitalized that her father took ill. His symptoms came on slowly, gradually, his skin paling, his body weight diminishing, and then his hair began falling out.'

'Arsenic?'

'In his tea, we believe.'

'And yet you never charged her?'

'We couldn't. The family had a cook. They had a maid. Even a live-in nurse for when the children came home for visits, which of course became exceedingly rare as the illness progressed. In short, Lexa was surrounded by other suspects. There was no way to link her to the poisoning. And to be honest, at the time, I wasn't entirely sure she was involved. I had placed more of my focus on the nurse, still feeling Lexa to be a victim of her father's evil-doings.'

To hear that Dagan Novak got his own justice didn't particularly bother Striker. 'So she got away with one.'

'Yes, she did. Then, when Lexa was nineteen, she met a man named Victor Devorak. He was a young man, a good-looking man, from an estimable background. Within one year of being married to Lexa, he also developed a strange unknown illness and eventually passed away. Lexa moved on, and within two

more years she had met and married another young man, also from a rich family. His name was Kavill Svaboda. He lasted longer than her previous husband – almost three full years. But then, four months after Lexa obtained her medical degree, he passed away from unknown causes.'

Striker said nothing as he thought things through. Most everyone around this woman had died, and her two sisters had ended up sick in mental hospitals. The diagnosis was schizophrenia, but he now wondered if Lexa had also played a role in that. He didn't know enough about the illness to speculate.

'So two husbands in just over, say, six years. And they died in a similar manner to her father. Did you bring her in for questioning?' Striker asked.

'Of course I did. After the death of both husbands. The woman was a star. Charming and open. Confident. Secure.'

'Like most psychopaths. Were there any more deaths after that?'

The inspector let out a tired sound. 'I wouldn't know. She disappeared. Just upped and left the country. And no matter how I tried to track her down, I could never find her. One of my contacts had traced her as far as Brussels, but it was an unconfirmed sighting. And after that, the trail went cold. Plus the woman in Brussels had been many months pregnant.'

'Lexa does have children.'

The inspector made a sad sound. 'That is a truly horrible thing.'

'How long ago was that sighting?'

'I'm not sure any more.' Twenty years? The inspector made an uncomfortable sound. 'It's odd . . . when my receptionist told me she had the police from Canada on the phone, Lexa was the first person I thought of.'

'Any advice you can give with this woman?'

'Only this, Detective. *Catch* her. Never let her escape. For there is one thing I learned above all else with Lexa Novak. She will never stop killing. She simply enjoys it too much.'

Eighty-Seven

With the conversation with the Czech police inspector finished, Striker hung up the phone and sat back in his chair. He thought of the Ostermann family.

Dr Erich Ostermann had been evasive and secretive from minute one, and now that they had discovered the man's sexual perversions, that those actions all made sense. As a whole, the world may have become more accepting of people's sexual preferences, but there was little doubt that the professionals and politicians Ostermann hung out with would be less than understanding should his sadomasochistic goings-on ever come to light.

As for Dalia and Gabriel, they had been oddballs from the start. Lexa was the one who had surprised Striker the most. When he had first met her, she had come across as the beautiful, trapped wife of a powerful and dangerous man. Striker had found himself wanting to help her, intrigued by her charms. He now found it frustrating to see how easily she had played him.

And he looked forward to capturing her.

He was deep in thought on this matter when his cell phone went off with a text message. He picked up the cell and looked at the screen. What he saw made his heart clinch. There was a message. From Larisa.

From: Logan, Larisa
Subject: Lost

The message was brief, to the point, and the underlying sense of panic was unmistakable:

I'm not going back to the hospital. Not ever. But I'm afraid, Jacob. I think someone's been watching me. This morning. A woman with dark eyes. She felt very . . . *off*. Everywhere I turned, she was there. And I'm scared. Part of me just wants to end it all. I don't know what I should do . . . I want to trust you, but . . .

The message ended there, and it tugged at Striker's heartstrings. Here was the woman who had been there for him during his darkest hours, and when hers had come, he had fallen way short of doing anything remotely helpful. He looked at the message details. It had been sent only two minutes ago.

Quickly, he typed back:

Larisa, wait! Where are you?

He waited for a long moment, but received no response. Bad thoughts flickered through his mind as he thought over her description.

A woman. With dark eyes.

Striker got on the phone with Bell, his service provider. He gave them his badge number and position, his phone number, and told them to trace the text sender. The technician was resistant at first, and Striker lost his temper.

'This is a matter of life and death,' he explained. 'I know your company policy – I've done this a hundred times. Now trace the

goddam call and tell me where it's coming from. Or if anything happens to this woman, I'll be sure to hold you criminally responsible. Not the goddam company, but *you*.'

The clerk made an uncomfortable sound, then asked him to hold. Seconds later, he came back on the line. 'The text is coming from the Whistler Blackcomb area,' he said. 'Any closer than that, I can't give you.'

'Can't, or won't?'

'*Can't*. It doesn't show up as anything more specific than that.'

Striker cursed. He hung up the phone without saying goodbye and went over his options. Whistler Blackcomb was a two-mountain ski resort a hundred kilometres from the downtown core, which translated into roughly a two-hour drive.

An hour fifteen, if he needed it to be.

By population, the resort was the largest in North America. Normal population ranged from a steady flow of ten to fifteen thousand, but with the post-Christmas ski season set to begin, the two main resorts were overflowing with triple that number. Not to mention the numerous villages that clustered in pods around the outer perimeter. Looking for someone there would be like finding the proverbial needle in the haystack.

He cursed out loud. Thoughts of alerting the other police jurisdictions flickered through his mind, but he wiped them away when he recalled the last fiasco with Bernard Hamilton of Car 87 at the coffee shop in Metrotown. If Larisa felt he had tried to trick her again, she would run. And that was something he just couldn't risk.

There was no other option.

He dialled Felicia. She picked up on the first ring.

'Lonely Man's Hotline.'

Normally the comment would have brought a smile to his lips. Not today. 'Where are you?' he said.

'Heading back from Burnaby,' she said. 'Should be less than five minutes. I got the report on Gabriel.'

'Good. You can read it over and explain the whole story to me when we're on our road trip.'

'Road trip? To where?'

'Whistler Mountain,' Striker said. 'We're going after Larisa.'

Eighty-Eight

How long it took for the feeling to return to his legs, the Adder had no clue. Time, as always, was unimportant to him. At first, there was only numbness below his waist, and then slowly, constantly, the feeling came. The pain grew. And with it came mobility. By the time he heard the front door open and close once more – the sign that the Doctor had again returned – he was finally able to stand.

Only then did he realize he was still completely naked. All his clothes were outside by the lake.

He moved from the den and the roaring gas fire back into the kitchen, where the Doctor was making herself a second cup of green tea. She kept her eyes straight ahead and did not so much as glance at him when he entered.

'You're going after the girl,' she said.

'The girl?'

'Larisa Logan.'

The words made him pause. 'She does not matter.'

The Doctor's reply was terse. 'Do not think, Gabriel. *Listen*. And follow orders.'

He said nothing, he just nodded slowly, and the Doctor continued.

'Larisa Logan is the only person that can connect us to the deaths.'

'But the police already know.'

'Proof and knowing are different matters.' The Doctor laughed out loud. 'Besides, they have to find us first, Gabriel. It's time for a new look for this family. A new identity that can never be traced – which is why I took the other DVDs. *Your* DVDs. They are more evidence connecting us.'

A strange sickness hit his stomach. 'My DVDs—'

'They are *destroyed*, Gabriel. And you will make no more of them. Do you understand me? You will make no more.'

'I will make no more,' he said softly.

'Good. Then we are understood. Now go get your clothes and get some rest and leave me be for a while. I have much to go over, much to plan. You have caused me quite a bit of work.' She took her cup and walked into the den.

The Adder watched her go. When she had disappeared from view, he opened the sliding glass door. Outside, the sky was greying over, darkening.

It made the lake look like charcoal.

He turned his eyes away from it and walked down the porch steps. When he reached the edge of the lake ice, he grabbed his clothes. On his way back to the cabin, he knelt by the steps, retrieved his disc – his beloved Disc 1 – and tucked it in between his folded pants and shirt.

Then he returned inside the cabin. He made his way up the stairs to the second floor. At the top, Dalia was waiting for him. Her eyes were wide and hollow, and wet with tears, as if ready to cry. She tried to speak to him, but nothing came out, and she covered her mouth with her hand.

The Adder did not respond. He brushed gently past her, into her room, and picked up her laptop.

Dalia took in a deep breath. '*Gabriel, no,*' she whispered.

But he did not listen.

He took the laptop with him and headed for his room. Once inside, he shut the door and made his way into the closet. He closed the doors behind him, powered on the computer and logged on.

Then he slid in the disc.

Eighty-Nine

As Striker made his way out through the front doors of the annexe, his cell phone went off. He looked down at the screen, saw the name *Sue Rhaemer*, and felt a jolt of hope. It was Central Dispatch. Maybe they had a hit on one of the Ostermanns. He answered the call and stuck the phone to his ear. 'Sue,' he said. 'What you got?'

She laughed softly. 'Calm down, Big Fella, nothing about the Ostermanns, so you can get rid of your hard-on.'

Striker felt his renewed optimism disintegrate. 'Then what's the occasion?' he asked, not bothering to hide the disappointment in his voice.

'The occasion is Bernard Hamilton,' Sue said.

That made Striker take notice. 'Bernard? Now what has the idiot done?'

Sue chuckled at that. 'Nothing too crazy, really. But it's strange. He keeps calling me up and asking me questions – about you.'

'About me?'

'And the case you're on. This one with Larisa Logan.'

Striker felt his fingers ball up. 'You didn't tell him anything, did you?'

'No, I told him to buzz off in my usual polite way. But he did pique my interest. So I got a little creative up here and ran his

GPS history. A weird thing came back – Bernard's position is the exact same as yours, and it has been all day long.'

Striker thought that over. 'Are you sure?'

'Hundred per cent. And it was the same yesterday. Wherever you put yourself out, he does, too. It's almost like he's been following you – or at least following your unit status, seeing where you went, then re-attending.'

'The devious little—'

Striker cut himself off. He couldn't believe his ears. The prick had no shame, and his motive was obvious. Bernard was planning on following their leads, then sneaking in and making the grab on Larisa right from under their noses. Not only was it a shitty thing to do to one of your fellow officers, but it was putting the woman at greater risk.

He had had enough.

'There's something wrong with that guy,' Sue said.

'Darlin', you don't know the half of it.'

'Bernard's not supposed to be using us to check up on you. Want me to do something about it? Speak to one of my superiors down here?'

'I'll deal with it myself,' Striker said. 'Though I might need your assistance, if you feel like helping me put the screws on him.'

'Shipwreck, you've come to the right girl.'

Striker smiled. 'I'll call back.'

He hung up the phone, and walked out on to Cordova Street. Felicia was already on the sidewalk, waiting for him with two cups of coffee in her hands. She handed him one, then took a quick look at his hard expression and lost her smile.

'What's wrong?' she asked. He told her everything he'd just learned about Bernard Hamilton, and she let out a worried sound. 'He's gonna screw up everything.'

Striker just shook his head and smiled at her.

'Here's what I need you to do.'

Fifteen minutes later, Striker parked on the corner of Burrard and Pender and waited for Felicia to get out. She hopped out of the car, closed the door, and stood ten feet away on the sidewalk, in a nook to get away from the wind. Once she was ready and gave him the thumbs up, Striker grabbed the radio mike. He depressed the plunger and spoke.

'Detective Striker to Radio,' he said.

Sue Rhaemer answered. 'Go for Radio.'

'Did you get that address I asked for?'

'The one for Logan?' she replied. 'Yes, I sent it to your screen.'

'Thanks,' Striker said. 'Can you get my partner to switch to the Chat channel?'

Sue Rhaemer raised Felicia over the air, and Felicia responded.

'Switching to Chat,' she said.

Striker ramped the radio up to the next level, and waited to hear Felicia come across the air. 'Felicia on Chat,' she said. He waited a few more seconds, to be sure that Bernard would be eavesdropping on the conversation. Then he depressed the plunger.

'Hey, Feleesh, where are you?' he asked.

'Fifth floor. Why?'

'Get down here. I know where Larisa is hiding out.'

'Awesome, where?'

'She's up in Shaughnessy. 5142 Osler Street. Apparently her aunt lives there and has been letting her hide out for the last two days. I've got confirmation she's there right now. We'll be pushing our way in. The chief wants this done ASAP and kept under wrap.'

'I'm coming down now,' Felicia said. 'Pick me up.'

'Will do,' Striker said. 'Leaving Chat.'

He ramped the radio channel from Chat back to Dispatch. Then he called the Central Dispatcher. Sue Rhaemer answered on the first ring. She was already laughing.

'Did it work?' he asked her.

'I'm checking his GPS now,' she said. 'And . . . Bernard is heading *due south*.'

Her reply made Striker smile. It was perfect.

He thanked Sue for her help, then said goodbye. Felicia returned to the car just as he hung up. She crashed down in her seat, giggling, and closed the door behind her.

'So?' she asked. 'You think he was listening?'

'Oh, he was listening. You can count on it.'

Striker put the car into Drive and headed west. They'd gone less than a block before Felicia spoke again. '5142,' she said thoughtfully. 'The Shaughnessy area? What's that Osler Street address for?'

Striker just grinned and kept driving.

'Trust me,' he said. 'You don't want to know.'

Ninety

'Whistler,' Felicia said again.

Striker nodded. 'Larisa's text was pinged there.'

He drove down Hastings Street towards the Stanley Park Causeway and, from there, the Lions Gate Bridge. Once into North Van, it was just one long winding Trans-Canada Highway stretch to the Whistler Blackcomb ski resort.

'Whistler or Blackcomb?' Felicia asked.

'I don't know yet, one of the villages.'

Felicia looked at him like he was crazy. 'You know how many people are up there right now, Jacob. The ski season's on, for God's sake. There'll be more than—'

'I know, Feleesh, I know. But she's up there. Without a doubt. What if something happens and we're all the way down here with no way to get to her? I can't think of any other choice we have at this point.'

'I can. It's called the Feds. They have units all over that area.'

Striker cast her a hot stare. 'Absolutely not. If Larisa thinks we've sent another cop after her, it's all over. I won't let that happen. We do this one on our own.'

Felicia said nothing for a moment, then shook her head. 'It's not our jurisdiction, Jacob. You have to get permission from Car 10.'

'You know as well as I do what Laroche will say.'

'We have to tell him, Jacob. He's the Road Boss.'

Striker felt his knuckles tighten on the wheel. 'Not this time, Feleesh.'

'I really think—'

He pulled over to the side of the road and slammed the steering column in Park. When he turned to face her, his adrenalin was starting. 'I'm not doing anything that's going to jeopardize my chance of getting Larisa back. You're right. Calling Car 10 is the protocol, but you know what? I'm not doing it. Because I know what Laroche's response will be. He'll get all the different jurisdictions involved, we'll have another boondoggle like we had at Metrotown, and the next thing you know Larisa will be gone forever. Well, forget that. I *owe* her this. And I'm more than willing to risk my career doing it. You can get out right now and I'll completely understand. But know this: *I am going.*'

He reached over and opened the door for her.

Felicia just looked back at him with a surprised look in her eyes. Then he saw the anger. For a moment, he thought she might actually leave. But then she grabbed the door and slammed it shut. 'We're not going to get there any faster if you leave the car in Park.'

Striker said nothing. He just got the car back on the road and drove down the highway.

Destination: Whistler Blackcomb ski resort.

They were just entering the district of West Vancouver when the conversation about Larisa Logan ended and Felicia finally got down to business with the Gabriel Ostermann file. She grabbed the thin folder and opened it up. Striker glanced over and saw a police report as well as an addendum from the Ministry of Children and Families.

'The file looks thin,' he noted.

'Well, in this case, less is more,' Felicia said. 'You ready for this?'

Striker nodded. 'Go.'

And she read through the report.

'This all took place ten years ago, just after Lexa and Dr Ostermann got married.'

'Gabriel must have been only eight years old,' Striker pointed out.

Felicia nodded. 'Which is why the Ministry of Children and Families was involved and also why it was privatized.' She turned through the pages. 'The file itself was a 911 call that was later changed to a Sudden Death call. As it turns out, the Ostermanns were away on vacation at a place called Lost Lake. Gabriel and his younger brother, William, were out playing in the snow.'

'William?' Striker asked.

Felicia nodded. 'Apparently Lexa had *two* children she brought into the marriage – Dalia, and William . . . Anyway, Gabriel threw a Frisbee to his brother and William missed it. The toy went over his head and landed on the lake.'

'Which was frozen at the time?'

Felicia nodded. 'Yeah, exactly. So the Frisbee lands on the ice. The kids had been warned by their parents not to go near the lake because winter was ending and the ice was too thin. Well, the kids never listened. Gabriel was the oldest and heaviest, so he stayed ashore. William was the youngest and the lightest, so he went out to get it.'

'And the ice broke,' Striker said.

'Yeah. The kid went right through. Worst thing is there was a chance to save him. Apparently, the boy managed to grab on to the edge of the ice and hang on for quite some time. He kept calling for someone to help him, kept calling out for his brother. But Gabriel just froze.'

'Wow, completely?'

'Damn near catatonic,' she replied. 'It was apparently all caught on video by one of the neighbour's surveillance systems. Gabriel couldn't bear to watch. So he turned away from the boy. Fell down in the snow. Covered up his ears with his hands.'

Striker pictured the moment in his mind. 'Jesus.'

'When help finally came, it was too late. William was dead. Sunk somewhere beneath the ice. And Gabriel was damn near catatonic.' She leafed through the pages of the report, shaking her head with sadness. 'The ministry was involved quite a bit after that. They've made many notes about Erich Ostermann's detached fathering skills and even more about Lexa's treatment of the boy. How she blamed him for William's death.'

Striker thought about this and nodded. 'Lexa was pregnant in Brussels,' he said. 'Maybe William was her only biological son. And Dalia was born from her marriage to Gerald Jarvis. Before she married Erich Ostermann.'

'What's your point?' Felicia asked.

'That they're a blended family.'

'They're a freak show is what they are,' Felicia said.

Striker nodded. 'With Lexa as a mother, how could they be anything but?' He thought of what it must have been like to be an eight-year-old child growing up under her evil care – an eight-year-old that she blamed for her only son's death. What life must have been like for Gabriel Ostermann was unthinkable. 'It makes me think that Gabriel is less mentally ill with any known psychological diagnosis and more . . . programmed into what he has become.'

'Lexa made him,' Felicia said. 'There's no doubt. The one question is, did his father know?'

'Dr Ostermann?' Striker scowled. 'How could he not? You saw how he treated the boy – like a subject, not a son. The man

was wilfully blind to it all. Had to be with all of them living there. Pride and power, just like with Lexa – till he got caught.'

Striker looked down at the file. He saw no attached envelopes.

'Where is the video?' he asked.

'That's the strange thing,' Felicia said. 'The neighbour swore they had one, but when the police went to collect it, the tape was gone. It just vanished, and was never found again.'

Striker frowned at that.

'Nothing vanishes,' he said.

The tape was still out there somewhere.

Ninety-One

An hour later, Striker looked in his rear-view mirror and saw Brandywine Falls behind them. The waterfall was hard to see in the five o'clock dimness. The entire canyon around them was a charcoal-grey colour, so deep it was all he could do to make out the treeline.

'We're getting close,' he said.

Felicia just nodded. 'And then what? We wait around for another call that might not even come? Or another email message she won't respond to?'

That irritated Striker. '*No*, we start hitting the pavement. You know, good old-fashioned, hard-nosed police work. We'll start with Whistler and make our way into Blackcomb. Show her picture around. See what we get.'

Felicia remained unconvinced. 'We don't know if she's even in one of the villages any more. She could be in one of the smaller towns around the perimeter. Or even headed back to Vancouver.'

'She's *here*,' Striker said. 'And if you can come up with a better way of locating her, then let me know. I'm all ears.'

They drove on through the swerving bends and rising hills in silence, Striker thinking of what lay ahead and any possible routes their investigation could take, and Felicia going over the computer files for the millionth time. When the traffic

thickened and Striker saw a sign that signalled Whistler Golf and Country Club ahead, he spoke.

'We're almost there.'

Felicia looked up from the computer screen. 'My eyes are going buggy from the screen and I feel carsick from all this reading. I need a coffee before we start. And some food. We haven't eaten a thing since this morning; aren't you hungry?'

Before Striker could respond, his cell went off. He snatched it up, looked at the screen and saw a number he didn't recognize. He pulled over to the side of the road, into one of the runaway lanes, and answered.

'Detective Striker.'

'Shipwreck,' came the reply, the voice deep and gruff. It took Striker but a second to recognize it as his old friend Tom Collins, previously from Financial Crime.

'Hey, Tommy, what's up?'

'Those names you gave me to run through our insurance databases,' he said. 'You jerking my chain here, or what?'

Striker thought of the list he'd given Collins. Every name and date of birth had been one of the people listed in Lexa Ostermann's folders.

'I don't follow,' he said.

Collins explained: 'I thought these were all supposed to be victims of identity theft.'

'They are. Why? What's the problem?'

'The problem is they're all *dead*. Every single one of them.'

Striker said nothing for a moment. 'There were over fifty people on that list. How many of them did you—'

'Every single one of them.'

'Jesus.' Striker gave Felicia a glance and saw the curiosity in her eyes. He ignored it for the moment and asked Tom, 'How? What was the manner of death?'

'All sorts, really. Accidents. Unexplained natural causes. A lot of suicides.'

Striker thought this over. 'And what kind of policies did they have?'

'That's where it gets interesting. They had good life insurance policies. *All* of them. Over half of the claims have already been paid out. I've done the math here. Accumulatively, we're talking twenty-four million dollars from fourteen different insurance providers. And like I said, nearly half the claims haven't been finalized.'

Striker let this information sink in. Twenty-four million. The number was staggering.

'I thought life insurance didn't cover suicide?' he said.

'That's a common misconception,' Collins replied. 'Life insurance doesn't cover suicide in the first two years, the reason being that most people who are truly suicidal aren't in a mindset to wait two years before doing themselves in. But if someone already had a policy, and two years later they killed themselves, yeah, it's usually completely covered.'

Striker sat there with the phone stuck to his ear and watched the tail lights of the cars passing by them along the highway. Little rectangles of red slowly disappearing into the night. As he watched them, he thought everything over.

Stolen identities. All the name-change forms. And twenty-four million dollars in life insurance money.

'You still there?' Collins asked.

'Can you give me the policy numbers and the names of the insurance companies?' Striker asked.

'No problem.' Collins began reading them out.

Striker wrote them down in his notebook, one by one. When they reached the fourteenth name, he stopped writing and looked up. Something occurred to him. He told Collins to hold on for a second, then turned to Felicia.

'Where's the folder we got from Mapleview?'

'Which folder?'

'The one from Lexa's office. With the medical billing codes.'

Felicia reached into the back seat and grabbed the red folder. When she opened it up, Striker saw the first page – the one with the long codes – and he made the connection.

He pointed to one of the lines.

10–14141ML–MG900412.

'Look at that,' he said. 'The first seven digits match Mandy Gill's life insurance policy number.'

Felicia looked at this and nodded. 'You're right. And the rest?'

Striker looked at the next two letters. 'ML – Manual Life, the insurance provider.'

'Shit, you're right,' she said. 'And look at the second half of the code – MG900412. MG . . . that would be Mandilla Gill. Followed by her date of birth. April twelfth, 1990.' She looked down the page. 'Jesus, she has them all listed right here. It's *ten* pages long.'

Striker nodded. He got back on the phone and told Collins he would have to get back to him. When he turned to face Felicia, he saw that she was sitting there with a troubled look on her face.

'What?' he asked.

She spoke, almost hesitantly. 'It looks like Lexa and Dalia and Gabriel have been stealing people's identities, taking out life insurance policies, and then, after systematically bankrupting the victims, murdering them for the insurance claims, but making it look like accidents and tragedies and suicides.'

Striker nodded. 'Complicated and devious, but yes.'

'I have a problem with that. With the theory . . . it doesn't make sense.'

'In what way?'

'*Why?* Why would they do this? By marriage, Lexa is part

owner of the EvenHealth programme. It has to generate hundreds of thousands of dollars per year. And she gets a percentage on every SILC class any other clinic runs. They have a Beamer and a Land Rover. A mansion in Point Grey.'

'And your point is?'

'She doesn't have to do this. She doesn't need the money. She's *loaded*.'

Striker looked back at her and shook his had. 'You're missing the point. It's not about money, Feleesh. It never was.'

'Then what *is* it about?'

'Domination, manipulation, control. Lexa is the one running this thing, and she has been for years. She *owned* Ostermann. And she's the reason why the kids are as screwed up as they are. She doesn't do this for the money. Or for security. Or for anything materialistic. She does it for the thrill of the hunt. She does it because she's a psychopath. A serial killer. And she lives for one thing and one thing only – the *game*.'

Ninety-Two

The Adder sat in the darkness of the closet with the laptop in his lap. Disc 1 ended, and he was filled with the heavenly bliss, that *peace* he felt every time he watched the video.

Disc 1.

William's Beautiful Escape.

Two hours ago, out by the lake, he had thought it was his turn for the Beautiful Escape. When the Doctor had injected him and he'd felt his body melt into the ice below, the darkness had been warm and overpowering. Heavy magnetic waves had pulled him towards places unknown.

But now he was here again. Back in this world.

Back in the cold.

The thought did not stir his emotions. Not much ever did.

But the Doctor had. Earlier in the day. With one injection, she had broken all boundaries between them. Wiped away the invisible lines. In essence, she had betrayed him.

The whole thing was bemusing to him.

The Adder had no idea how many victims the Doctor had killed in what she called her 'business'. And he didn't really care. He knew the truth. This entire process was not a business, but a *game* to her – one of dominance and power and sadistic need. With every fresh death, she seemed to climb one more rung on that ladder in her mind.

But the joke was on her, because the Adder knew one thing about the game that the Doctor did not – there was no end to that ladder. It just went on for ever and ever and ever. Which left them with this demonic game they played. Just Gabriel and Mother; just the Adder and the Doctor.

In a never-ending game of Snakes & Ladders.

The thought made the Adder feel bad emotions again, so he leaned forward and hit Play, and once again William's Beautiful Escape played out on the LED screen. The converted video was old and poor in quality. There was only static for sound. But that did not diminish it at all.

The Adder watched the young boy fall through the ice, and he saw himself there too – also just a boy – shaking, trembling, crying hysterically, then crumbling to the ground with his hands over his ears. Unable to look. Unable to face what was happening.

Unable to run for help.

Back then, this moment had been his own personal Hell on Earth; but over time – over several hundred viewings of the feed – the Adder had come to see the truth behind the moment. The reality. The only real importance.

Death; it was the only reason for living.

And William had been released from the chains of this cold world. He had been set free from this Hell. Utterly, totally free.

The Adder watched the screen with his eyes turning wet as the emergency workers came rushing in and pulled his little brother from the lake. His body was soaked, his skin as white as any angel. Inside his blood and meat were frozen, but his soul was soaring, soaring, *soaring* far away from here.

'You're free,' the Adder whispered. 'Fly away, little bird. Fly away.'

The film ended, and suddenly there was a blinding brightness.

The Adder raised his hands. Looked up at the closet door. And knew what had happened before his eyes even adapted.

The Doctor had found him.

Ninety-Three

From the runaway lane where Striker and Felicia were parked, the drive to the Whistler Blackcomb ski village was less than twenty minutes. Before pulling back on to the Sea-to-Sky Highway, Striker thought of Lexa and Larisa. What were the odds they would both be here in the village?

Not likely. And yet here they were.

A woman with dark eyes. That was what Larisa had texted.

The more he thought about it, the more he feared that finding Larisa might be as simple as finding Lexa. For they were both after Larisa. In a race – one Striker didn't want to enter.

Lexa was an expert in finding her victims.

And that worried him.

Striker scanned through the notes he'd made on the files. They clearly showed that Lexa's victims fell into one of two categories. They were either the marginalized people in society – the sex-trade workers, the mentally ill, the poor, the secluded and alone.

Or they were the extremely well-to-do – victims who had good jobs. Victims who had money. And extremely good credit. Victims who had been carefully selected, because they had no family. No friends. People whose entire life was work. People who no one would bother to worry about if they went missing or passed away from an unexpected tragedy.

Striker took the box from the back seat and passed it to Felicia.

'I've been through these already,' she said.

'Not like this,' he said. 'Go through the files one more time, but this time look for victims who had *status*.'

'Status? Why?'

'Because with status comes money. When you get the top ten or fifteen income earners, run their name through the property registries and see if any of them owned property up in Whistler or Blackcomb.'

Felicia's eyes took on an excited look. 'One of them was another doctor,' she noted. 'And one was a lawyer, I think.' She opened the box and started pulling files.

Striker drove back on to the highway and continued north towards the village. Ten minutes later, Felicia had compiled a list of the twelve most well-off victims. She got on the phone with her contact at the land registrar's office, and began making notes. By the time Striker drove around the last curve of road and saw the bright halo lights of the ski resort, Felicia had already finished narrowing down their targets.

'We got three,' she said. 'Four, if you count the lawyer who owned a cabin back in Furry Creek.'

Furry Creek. Striker was frustrated to hear that; they'd passed Furry Creek Golf Course over thirty minutes ago. To backtrack now would waste more time. 'What about the other three?' he asked.

'All up here,' she said.

'A guy named Robinson – he was a stockbroker – owned a cabin right up on the mountain. In Whistler Creekside, on Nordic Avenue. The next guy, a man named Bellevue – he had old family money – lived on Panorama Trail. Last person's name is Sutton. He lived just off the main drag.'

Felicia pulled out her iPhone and opened Google Maps.

'These cars should have satellite navigation built into them,' she griped.

'Welcome to city funding,' Striker replied. 'Just start querying.'

'Which one first?'

'Whichever is closest,' Striker said. 'And hurry up. We've finally arrived.'

Ninety-Four

'I *knew* it!'

As the Doctor stood above the Adder, looking down on him, the mask she wore crumbled once again, revealing the monster that lay behind it. Without thinking, the Adder closed the laptop and hit the Eject button.

'The moment I saw the other DVDs, I knew you had more,' the Doctor spat. '*Give it to me.*'

The Adder felt his heart hammer inside his chest.

'No,' he said.

The laptop's DVD player ejected out the disc. The Adder gently took it from the DVD tray and tried to place it back in the case; before he could, the Doctor reached forward and snatched it from his hands.

'I'm *destroying* this thing once and for all!'

'No,' he said.

And now there was a tightness spreading throughout his chest. Into his lungs. Into his heart. A strange empty feeling ballooning inside him.

'NO!'

But the Doctor refused to listen.

She stormed out of the room with his precious DVD in her hand. It was his one and only copy, with the original lost – his

last connection to William – and this time the Adder did what he had never done before.

This time, the Adder *acted*.

Ninety-Five

The search for the first of the three properties ended as quickly as it began. The first place, a private cabin previously owned by David Sutton, had been bulldozed to make way for a new set of condominiums that were already being sold as timeshares.

From there, they drove across the small village to the address for a man named Reginald Robinson. They'd barely set up on the place when a grey Audi Q7 pulled into the driveway, and a family piled out.

Striker spent less than a minute watching them unload their snowboarding gear before realizing this was another dead end. He approached the father, showed the man his badge and credentials, and explained that they were looking for Reginald Robinson.

The man's response was direct. 'He doesn't live here. Hell, we just bought the place last summer.'

'Do you mind me asking from who?' Striker asked.

'A doctor from the City.'

'Dr Ostermann?'

The man nodded, and his face took on a nervous look. 'Yes, I believe that was his name. Is everything all right? Should I be concerned?'

'You're fine,' Striker said. 'Thank you for your time.'

They left Robinson's lot and drove to the last place on their

list. As they made their way there, Striker felt a sense of futility wash over him. The last address they had was slightly farther out, on the east side of the village. If it was negative, they had nothing. It would be canvass time.

Not five minutes later, the road turned from asphalt to gravel, and they came to a T in the road. The right lane turned back towards the highway; the one to the left turned from gravel to hard-packed dirt, and ran straight.

Striker looked down that way. With the night fully cloaked and a fog brooding through the trees, all he could see was a mass of blackness, with the odd porch light piercing the haze. He parked the car on a small outcrop of gravel on the side of the road, then took out his flashlight and shone it all around the road, looking for a street sign. He could find none.

'Google Maps says this is it,' Felicia said. 'Panorama Trail.'

He nodded. 'It's desolate.'

'If we drive in, anyone there will see us coming a mile off.'

Striker agreed. Walking in was the best choice.

They got out and started up the trail.

The man who lived here before his death was Luc Bellevue. No transfer of property form had ever been filed, so by all accounts the place should have been used by his remaining family.

Striker and Felicia followed the bend of the road.

On the left side, a small lake appeared that was backed by tall thick trees that looked completely black in the night-time shadow. The air above the lake was dark and seemed clouded in mist. Everything was very, very quiet.

They marched on. A hundred metres later, around the long curve of lake, a cabin came into view. It was small. Quaint. Made of logs. It sat on the north side of the lake and backed right down to the shoreline.

When they reached the front of the cabin, most of the windows were dark and had the drapes pulled tightly across. Striker spotted movement in one of them. It was fast and fleeting, but it was there. Someone was home.

Ninety-Six

The Adder found the Doctor downstairs in the study.

'Please,' he said. '*PLEASE!*'

It was the tenth time he had begged her. He knew of nothing else to say.

She walked past him into the kitchen, a smile stretching her lips and her ice blue eyes holding him in their grip. It was as if she was enjoying this moment, *relishing* it. And the Adder knew that she was. Cruelty had always been one of her strongest traits.

'I need it,' he said.

The Doctor made no immediate response. She just stared at him for a long moment, and the smile slowly fell from her lips. Her eyes darkened. Her jaw turned tight. 'You *disgust* me,' she finally said. '*You* should have been the one who died that day, not my precious William. *He* would have learned. *He* would have listened. *He* would never have caused the damage that you have caused us.'

She held the disk delicately between her long fingers. When her eyes met the Adder's – when the faintest hint of a smirk formed at the corners of her cruel mouth – he understood full well her intention.

'No, please! *NO!*'

But his cry meant nothing.

The Doctor tightened her grip and snapped the disc in two.

And the Adder let loose a howl that filled the room. He lashed out and grabbed the Doctor by the wrist, and bent it backwards. She let out a cry, half of surprise and half of pain. She tried to pull away from him. When he did not let her, she raised her free hand and smacked him across the face — a hard, full-forced *SLAP!*

He did not so much as flinch.

'I wish you were never born,' she spat. 'I wish your whore of a mother had drowned you at birth — then my William would still be alive!'

'William is dead,' the Adder said. 'He has been for a very long time.'

Her eyes narrowed. 'You have never been anything but a wretched, pathetic failure, Gabriel. And a poor excuse for a son.'

The words were meant to hurt, but they had no effect on him. The Adder took them all in, thought them over . . . and then he nodded strangely.

'But I'm not your son, am I?' he said.

'What?'

'I am my *father's* son. And you are no longer his wife. You are not my mother. Not any more.'

'How *dare* you!' She slapped him across the face again, across the same stinging red mark that already marred his skin, and broke away from him. When he offered her no real reaction, but only smiled, she reared from him.

'You stay back,' she ordered.

'You're not my mother.' He stepped towards her.

'I said, stay back! I *order* you to stay back. You will listen to me. I am your doctor, Gabriel! Your *DOCTOR!*'

The Adder reached out and wrapped his long fingers around Lexa's slender throat.

'The game is over, Doctor,' he said. '*You lose.*'

Ninety-Seven

Striker stepped off the dirt road on to one of the trails that snaked through the heavily forested area and paralleled the lake. Moving slowly and through shadow, he hoped to be hidden. When he and Felicia moved forward, making their way on to the private lot, they heard arguing inside the cabin.

He stiffened at the sound. He turned and looked at Felicia.

'Male and female?' he asked.

'It *sounds* like it, but I can't tell for sure.' Felicia crept up to the window and peered inside. 'I can't see anything. Let's just go in and get them.'

Striker motioned her back. 'Not yet.'

'Why not?'

'Because we don't know who's in there yet. If Gabriel or Dalia or Lexa are in there, or if they come up the road and spot us, they'll run. They'll get away. And they'll never stop killing. We need *containment*.'

Felicia agreed. 'Then call in the Feds. The Whistler Police has units ten minutes away from here. Get them here and we can cordon off the whole house.'

Striker thought this over. 'If Lexa or Gabriel or Dalia see them, they'll take off and be gone again, and this time maybe for good.'

'They can use plainclothes cops.'

Striker frowned. The talk had gone full circle, back to square one. A decision had to be made. He took out his phone, being careful to block the light of the screen with his body, and called 911. All he got was a dropped signal. He put the phone away.

'No reception,' he said.

The decision had been made for them.

He pointed to the southwest corner of the cabin. 'Cover that. Scream if you need me and I'll come running.'

Felicia just tightened her grip on her SIG and slowly made her way through the trees, around to the other side of the house. She'd barely been gone a minute when Striker detected a lone figure walking up the road: average height, long black hair, slender build.

Dalia.

Striker watched her as she walked up the road towards the cabin, then crossed the yard. Even in the darkness, he could see that her face was tight and lost. Something was wrong; he could feel it.

Ninety-Eight

The Adder stood outside on the frozen grass, his hot breath fogging up the cold night. Small bits of broken ice covered the toes of his runners, and the bottom of his pants legs were wet. In front of him, her upper body submerged face down in the freezing water of the lake, was the Doctor.

He looked down at her body and felt nothing. Because it was nothing.

Just a bad roll of the dice.

Behind him, the soft *swish* of a sliding door could be heard, and then there were footsteps on the deck. He didn't bother to turn around. It was Dalia, he knew. Coming back again after running away – as she had done so many times before. Escape and return. Escape and return. Escape and return.

It was her life.

'Gabriel?' she asked.

Her steps came closer, and suddenly there was a gasp.

'GABRIEL! Oh no! Oh no! Oh no! Oh no! What have you done, Gabriel? *What have you DONE!*'

She screamed and then screamed some more. He said nothing to her. He did not so much as look in her direction. And seconds later, he heard her run off. Somewhere around the house. In that moment, he had lost her. She was gone. And he would never see her again.

Go after her.

It was a soft thought in his head, a whisper from the angels.

But he did not. He could not. For there were other plans now. And they were all that mattered. Running after Dalia would be changing the goal of the game – and that was the one thing that could never be changed. He had no choice in the matter; the rules were long written.

It was sad. On some deeper level, he knew this.

But what did that matter? He now wondered . . . had there ever been a choice? Perhaps it was always meant to be this way. Fated. Perhaps tonight's game would even lead to his own death.

The thought was enthralling. If Death did come, he was prepared for it. He accepted it. He was *happy* for it. At last, his own time. His own Beautiful Escape. And he smiled because either way he would win this game – in the biggest release of his life when he freed Jacob Striker from this world, or in his own release from this torment. Either way, he was ready. Ready for the final throw of the dice. And why not? Nothing could last forever.

All games eventually came to an end.

Ninety-Nine

It happened fast. One moment, Striker was trying to move to a better position in order to see what all the screaming was about; the next moment, he saw Dalia racing around the house. She plunged through the trees away from him.

A second later, Felicia went racing after the girl.

'Stop!' Felicia called. 'Vancouver Police, Dalia! STOP!'

In one brief moment, both women were swallowed by the darkness.

Striker started after them.

He got only a few feet before coming to a hard stop. There was no doubt that whoever was inside the cabin – Gabriel, Lexa or both of them – now knew of the police presence. If Striker went racing after Dalia, then Lexa and Gabriel would be free to escape. Maybe this time forever.

He was torn.

Felicia needed him. But if he allowed Lexa and Gabriel to escape, there was no telling how many more victims they would kill. Maybe not here, but in another town. Another province. Another country. Everywhere Lexa went, she left a trail of death in her wake. And over the years, she'd programmed Gabriel into being the Adder. All in all, it made one thing clear.

'They have to be stopped.'

At any cost.

Striker turned back towards the cabin. It looked smaller now. Secluded and empty. Almost all the inside lights were off, and from this new location, Striker could hear the *chug-chug-chug* of the generator running out back.

Where Dalia had run from.

Striker readied his pistol, then made his way around the lot towards the back of the cabin. He reached the corner of the house, raised his pistol and peered around the edge. Everything there was quiet and the lake was eerily still. Fog floated across the water and through the trees like a living beast, so thick that Striker could not see across the lake. Out there, across the thin ice, there was only a rolling mass of cold murky blackness.

But no Lexa.

And no Gabriel.

Striker rounded the corner and made his way towards the cabin. The sliding glass door was wide open and the kitchen light was on. He walked up the slippery wooden steps of the porch, came flush with the entrance, and looked around the area.

No one was there to be seen.

He stepped forward into the kitchen and listened to the sound of his shoes against the hard tiles of the floor. Slowly, cautiously, he made his way through the first floor, and then the second.

The place was empty.

They were gone.

Frustrated, he made his way back outside. He stood on the porch and shone his flashlight around the lake. At first he saw nothing.

Then he discovered the body.

It was a few feet out from the edge, where the ice thinned and turned to freezing lake water. As he closed in on it, he saw that

it was lying face down. He crouched low, reached out with one hand, and grabbed hold of the arm. When he flipped it over, a sense of desperation filled him.

It was Lexa.

The Adder had killed her. He was spiralling out of control. And he was gone.

One Hundred

The voices were back, the laughter and giggles echoing in his head. But this time, the Adder managed to control them. He had lost his most precious of all precious videos and he did not have the headphones he needed for his iPhone, so he could not even listen to the white noise.

It did not matter.

A new sense of control filled his body. Electric. Empowering. Like ice water in his veins. Ever since breaching the line – ever since killing the Doctor – a sense of invulnerability had filled him. He was unstoppable.

Completely, utterly, one hundred per cent *unstoppable*.

And he nearly laughed out loud as he realized that.

He moved slowly through the wooded grove. Speed was not necessary. What mattered here was silence. Stealth. Besides, there was little point in running through the forest blind. Broken ankles were bad for the killing business.

As he walked steadfastly, thoughts of Jacob Striker filled his head. The big detective had looked so determined back at the cabin, so intense and powerful. The Adder had watched him from the shadows, impressed.

It had been foolish to do so – he should have been gaining as much ground between them as he could. But something about the detective intrigued the Adder. The man had a magnetic presence.

Like a tar pit sucking him down.

He headed straight north and, when he found the proper trail, increased his speed towards Green Lake. That was where Striker would eventually find him. It was a certainty. Because the Adder knew something important that no one else had known – not Detective Striker or Detective Santos or even the omnipotent Doctor herself. He knew where Larisa Logan had been hiding.

And he was determined to get there before Striker.

One Hundred and One

'Felicia!' Striker called out.

It was the tenth time he'd screamed her name, but to no avail, and now he was beginning to panic. He made his way back to the main road. Once there, he tried her cell again. The signal was weak, but the call went through, and it was picked up on the second ring.

'Jacob?' she asked.

'Jesus, you scared the shit outta me. Where the hell are you?'

'I'm back in the village. She ran here. But I've lost her.'

He was angry now. 'I didn't know if you were dead or lying in the forest somewhere. I've been looking everywhere for you!'

'I'm sorry,' she said. 'Are you okay?'

'I'm fine.'

'And Gabriel?' She asked the question almost tentatively.

'Gone. He killed Lexa.'

Felicia made a shocked sound. 'My God.'

'He's spinning out of control, Feleesh. Gone right off the deep end. And he knows we're here after him. No point in hiding that any more. Call the Feds. We need more units. We got to catch this guy before he escapes. I'll meet you back in the village. By the flag pole in the centre square.'

'Okay. I'll call the Feds right now.'

'And, Feleesh. Be careful on this one. We've lost sight of them, but that doesn't mean they've run off.'

'I can take care of myself, Jacob. Just get here.'

The line went dead and Striker started hiking back towards the cruiser. He'd gone less than ten feet when his phone vibrated again. He snatched it up, expecting to see Felicia's name on the screen, but instead he saw that he had another text message. The send time was only a minute ago. He opened it up, saw Larisa's name, and read the text:

Jacob, R U there?

He immediately typed back.

I'm here. Where are you?

After a moment, she responded:

I have proof, Jacob. A video. The doctors at Mapleview are killing people for money.

You need to come in.

They'll send me back to Riverglen. To the doctor.

I won't let them. I'll be with you.

He received no response, so he typed back:

Larisa? U there?

You can't stop them. And I can't take this any more.

Let me help you!

Striker waited for a long moment, so long he thought Larisa had ended the conversation. But finally a text came back:

> I'm so tired, Jacob. I'll leave you the video I have of Sarah. No. 5 Old Mill Road. I hope it helps you stop them. Thanks for being my friend.

Striker got a bad feeling from her text. He recalled her PRIME files, remembered her emotional instability. He typed back:

> Don't do anything foolish, okay? I'm coming right now!

No response.

> Larisa?

Nothing again.

Striker sprinted back down the trail to the cruiser. Once there, he punched the address into Google Maps and located it. He started the engine. Hit the gas. And left a trail of dirt and gravel in his wake.

Old Mill Road was only minutes away.

One Hundred and Two

Striker drove so fast he almost lost control of the cruiser on the icy gravel. When he reached Old Mill Road, he floored it. The road was narrow and old, unpaved. Tall rows of cedars and Douglas firs bordered the road, blocking out any of the weak moonlight that managed to struggle through the heavy blanket of fog.

The road was a strip of blackness.

He spotted a house at the end. Even in the pale glow of the cruiser's headlights, the place looked ramshackle. Old. And dark. All the lights were off and the front door was wide open.

Striker wasted no time. He jumped out of the cruiser, taking out his flashlight and pistol at the same time.

He reached the front door, used the frame for cover, and flashed his light inside. Everything was dark and still and empty. He hit the light switch, but nothing happened. And he realized there were no sounds coming from the generator.

'Larisa?' he called out. 'Larisa, it's Jacob – are you here?'

When he received no response, he made the decision. There was no more time for delay. Flashlight illuminating the way, gun aimed ahead, finger alongside the trigger, Striker stepped into the darkness.

He moved quickly, not allowing himself to slow for even a

second. He made his way out of the small foyer, through the living room, kitchen, den and then the bedroom.

But there was no sign of her.

He took the stairs into the basement more slowly, keeping his body tight to the wall. When he reached the bottom and his shoes touched the hard concrete of the cellar floor, he scanned the area around him and spotted a long narrow hallway. There was a doorway to the right and one straight ahead at the far end of the hall.

The doorway on the right was open; the one at the end was closed.

Striker moved forward to the first doorway. He stopped and aimed his flashlight into the room, illuminating all four corners.

And that was when he found her.

Slumped in a chair at the far end of the room was the woman he had been searching for these last three days.

'*Larisa!*' he said.

He moved forward through the darkness. Came to within ten feet of her. And stopped hard. Her head was turned down and her eyes were half open. Dangling from her right hand was an empty pill case, and at her feet was a DVD case with the name *Sarah Rose* on it. Striker gently placed two fingers against her neck and felt for a pulse. She was warm, but he could feel no beating of her heart.

'Please, Larisa,' he said. 'Please.'

He was running out of time.

One Hundred and Three

Desperation flooded him. Striker took out his cell to call 911; it rang on him before he could even dial. He stuck it to his ear.

'Striker,' he said.

'Where are you?' Felicia asked.

'Number five Old Mill Road,' he said. 'No time for talk. I got Larisa here. She's overdosed on pills. Call 911 for an ambulance and get your ass up here now.'

He hung up without waiting for a response, then grabbed Larisa and placed her on the floor, so he could begin CPR. Keep her heart going till the medics got here.

His phone vibrated again. He looked down and read the words:

I have proof, Jacob. I'm scared.

I have proof, Jacob. I'm scared

I have proof, Jacob. I'm scared.

;O)

He stood back up, momentarily confused. 'What the hell?'

And his phone went off with another text:

Congratulations, Hero, you found her – or have I found you?
Snake eyes!
SNAKE EYES!
SNAKE EYES!

One Hundred and Four

Striker tore his eyes away from the text, knowing for certain the Adder was here. He placed his back to the wall, moved slowly to the corner of the room, and kept scanning with his flashlight and gun. With the exception of him and Larisa, the room was empty. Dark. Quiet.

There was only one way in, and only one way out.

For a moment, he considered staying put. Keeping all his attention on the doorway and waiting for back-up. Then he heard a door slam out front. Thoughts of being trapped in another inferno flashed through his mind, as did the notion of Gabriel Ostermann escaping once more.

He got moving.

Gun aimed ahead of him, flashlight illuminating the way, Striker made his way back across the room and turned towards the front foyer. The door leading out front was just a stairway away.

It was closed.

Striker took a step towards it, then heard a shuffling sound behind him. He stopped and slowly turned around. He looked back down the hallway. On the right side was the doorway into the room where Larisa's body lay on the floor. At the far end was the only other room the basement owned. The door there had been closed when he'd first come down the stairs.

Now it was open.

He moved to one side of the hall, out of the main line of fire, and took aim on the open doorway. He called out:

'Vancouver Police, Gabriel. I know you're here and I've got every reason to believe you're armed and dangerous. Come out with your hands where I can see them and you won't get hurt.'

No response.

Striker listened for a moment, heard nothing else. He slowly left his position of cover and made his way down the hall. When he came to within ten feet of the open doorway, he shone his flashlight inside the room.

From the cover of the door frame, the weak beam of his flashlight caught a vague shape. Someone was hiding in a small nook of the wall. In the closet. He took aim on the figure and called out once more:

'I see you, Gabriel. Don't move!'

But the figure only turned slightly and shuffled out of view; as it moved, Striker caught a brief glimpse of the man's face. There was no doubt about it.

It was Gabriel.

The Adder.

'I said, don't move, Gabriel!' Striker ordered again.

When the Adder disappeared from Striker's line of fire, Striker seized the moment before it was lost. He moved forward, ready to fire. It wasn't until he had stepped right into the room that he realized his mistake. What he was staring at wasn't a closet; it was the wall. And as he looked at the wall, he saw a poster on it – but the writing was all *backwards*.

Then he realized. It was not a wall but a full-length mirror.

The Adder was *behind* him.

He spun to the right just as he felt an arm wrap around his neck from behind. There was a sharp pinprick and, almost

immediately, a numbing sensation ran from his neck through-out the rest of his body, snaking out like long pulsating tendrils.

Striker shoved back, but it was too late. He felt his body melting on him. His legs gave out. And he went down firing.

He hit the floor hard. Felt the air explode from his lungs. And watched the darkness sweeping into his sight from all corners of his periphery. He thought of his daughter, Courtney, and then of Felicia and Larisa, whose life depended on him escaping this moment.

But the last image Striker saw, as he was sucked down by the heavy blackness, was that of Gabriel. The Adder was staring back at him, his pale twisted expression the only visible beacon for him in a dark and cold vacuum.

One Hundred and Five

First came the sound.

There was a faint, wailing noise in the background, like the soft banshee cries of some strange beast coming to take him away. The wail grew louder and louder until it was right on top of him – an overbearing echo in his ears. Until Striker realized the source of the call:

Sirens.

Striker tried to open his eyes, and then he realized they were already open. The strange supple warmth slowly washed away from him and was replaced by a stark coldness. The darkness slowly ebbed away, and Striker looked up to see three people on top of him.

Two men dressed in white . . .

Paramedics.

And one between them. A face that made him smile and relax and brought back all the warmth that had been stolen from his body.

'Feleesh,' he said. His voice sounded weak and very far away.

'Just relax, Jacob,' she said. 'They're giving you some drugs. You need to stay still.'

He tried to get up; she pushed him back down.

'You need to *relax*.'

'Larisa . . .'

'They got her, too, Jacob. She's breathing and en route to Whistler hospital.'

He let go. Felt his body melt into the floor. And he lazily looked left.

Lying on his back was Gabriel Ostermann. Two other paramedics, both women, were hovering over the Adder, examining his chest and stomach area. In the centre of the two was a large meaty hole. Striker saw this glistening redness and the vague recollection of past gunfire returned to his ears.

His bullets had found their target.

Centre mass.

The simple action of looking at the Adder drained him, and Striker let his head fall back to the floor. He looked up, straight ahead at Felicia, who was hovering like an earthbound angel. Behind her, one of the female paramedics let out a surprised sound.

'Jesus, this guy's still alive,' she said.

And Striker realized they were talking about Gabriel Ostermann.

'He keeps whispering,' one of the women said to her partner. 'I can't make it out. What the hell's he saying? *I'm the Villain?*'

Striker understood the word, and he breathed heavily as he spoke.

'He said *William* . . . he said, *I'm coming, William.*'

And then the medications pulled him under and he did not wake for a long time.

EPILOGUE

One Hundred and Six

It was a grey Sunday morning – over twenty-four hours since the Adder had injected him with mivacurium chloride – and Striker still felt like he had a hangover. A steady *thud-thud-thud* drummed behind each temple like a second steady pulse that was impossible to ignore.

He was thankful that Homicide was empty.

The coffee brewing was fresh. He poured himself a cup of it and swallowed three painkillers – the sting of the burn would not go away. He wandered back through the rows of empty cubicles to his desk. Open on the desktop were four separate reports. The first one was the statement he was required to deliver to the Police Board regarding the Billy Mercury situation. This was mandatory for all police shootings. The report was almost done, but Striker was still unsure about the wording in a few lines. With his head as messed up as it was, having an agent from the Union look it over wasn't a bad idea.

He saved the file for later.

The other three reports were all linked because they had to do with Gabriel Ostermann. The first of the three reports was for Mandy Gill's murder. The second was for Sarah Rose's. And the third was for Larisa's attempted murder. There were undoubtedly dozens more charges coming, but none of them could be laid until all the proper paperwork had been gone through and

all investigative ends tied. Knowing Gabriel was responsible for other murders was not enough to charge the man; they needed reasonable grounds. Evidence.

Striker blinked a few times as his eyes dried up. There was so much to do. So much to tie in. It would have been easier if Gabriel Ostermann had died. But the man had not. He had hung on until the ambulance crew got him to Whistler Medical Center, and since then his condition had been upgraded from critical to stable.

It concerned Striker. The man was going to live, and given his mental health status, there had already been rumblings from the Crown as to whether he was mentally fit to stand trial when he recovered from his injuries. The thought of the Adder ever being released again was a realistic concern.

And that was to say nothing of Dalia. The girl had vanished in the ski resort village. Striker had no idea where she had gone, but he did know this – she was out there somewhere and she was dangerous.

The whole situation gave him chills. Then again, maybe it was more the after-effects of the injection the Adder had given him.

He tried not to think about it. There was still a lot of work to do. So he buried his head in the computer and kept pounding away at the keys. He was so focused on the work, he barely heard the office door open behind him. Only when it slammed shut did he bother to turn around.

What he saw made him smile.

Standing in the doorway was Bernard Hamilton. His face was so red it matched the ruby silk dress shirt he wore. He stormed across the office, his ponytail swinging behind him, and stopped a few feet short of Striker's desk.

'Nice shirt,' Striker said. 'When did you go colourblind?'

Bernard just glared at him.

'You think that stunt you pulled the other day was funny?' he asked. 'I could have lost my job.'

Striker wheeled his chair around to face the man. 'Do I think what was funny?'

'You know damn well what – sending me to Osler Street. That was Laroche's house, for fuck's sake! I stormed right in on his wife's birthday party.'

'Did she like the present you brought her?'

Bernard's eyes narrowed. 'This could cost me my chance at Cop of the Year, Striker! You know Laroche is on the board. He'll never pick me now. You did this on purpose!'

Striker leaned back in his chair and nodded. 'Really? Because I don't remember *telling* you anything. How did you come across that address – another source?' When Bernard said nothing back, Striker continued. 'You know, I can't help thinking that there's a moral to the story here somewhere. Something to do with honesty maybe. I dunno, I'll think about it.'

Bernard said nothing for a moment, and the crimson colour extended up past his forehead and on into his bald spot. His jaw turned hard and he extended his chin as he spoke.

'I won't forget this,' he said.

Striker put his feet up on the desk and gave Bernard his best smile. 'That's funny,' he said. 'Because I already have.'

Hamilton stormed out of the office, and Striker watched him go. Suddenly, his headache was better and the coffee tasted fresher. He smiled as he sipped it.

It was almost like the sun had come out.

One Hundred and Seven

An hour later, Striker and Felicia walked down the long hallway of the east-end section of the Riverglen Mental Health Facility. They reached Dr Ostermann's office, made a sharp left, and walked into the common room where patients were milling about in groups by the backgammon table, TV, and fireplace.

'This is a good thing you're doing,' Felicia said.

'It's just something I have to do,' he replied.

She smiled at him, reached across his arms, and stole a package of chocolates from the box he was carrying. She'd barely pocketed the candy before Striker found the man he was looking for, playing cards in a group of four.

'Morning, Henry,' he said softly.

The patient in the pale blue hospital clothes turned slowly around in his seat. One look at Striker and his face tensed. 'You're DANGEROUS!' he yelled, and immediately stood up and clenched both his hands into fists.

In the far corner, the guard stood up from the table, but Striker waved him down.

'I'm not dangerous today, Henry,' Striker explained. He slowly pulled his jacket out of the way, revealing his side and showing that there was no gun holstered to his belt. 'You showed me how wrong I was the other day, so I just wanted to come by

and say thank you for teaching me that. And also to say I'm sorry if I upset you.'

Henry said nothing for a long moment, then his expression relaxed a little. His posture deflated and he rubbed his nose. 'That's okay then . . . I guess.'

'Here, Henry. I got you something.'

Striker held out the box.

When Henry looked guardedly inside the box and saw the rows of yellow M&M packages, his face brightened.

'Peanut!' he said.

'Of course,' Striker said. 'Peanut's the best.'

Henry let out an excited gasp and grabbed the box. Laughing, he sat back down and began passing out M&M packages to his card-playing friends. Within seconds, he forgot that Striker and Felicia were even there.

'You ready?' Felicia asked.

Striker nodded. 'Let's go.'

They left the common room and made their way back down the grey halls of the facility. As they went, Felicia tore open the package of M&Ms she'd pilfered and popped a few in her mouth. She held up her hand and showed Striker her palm.

'Melt in your mouth, not in your hands.'

He grinned. 'You, or the M&Ms?'

She gave him a wry look and laughed.

Outside, the sun was out, high in the centre of the blue sky, and the wind was whipping in hard from the river. It blustered on as they climbed into the cruiser and drove out of the parking lot. When they were back on the freeway, heading for Vancouver, Felicia spoke again.

'Feel better?' she asked him.

'Yeah, I do,' he said, then added: 'I guess you're right. Chocolate does make everything better.'

One Hundred and Eight

They returned home at twelve noon. There was still a shitload of work to be done on all the reports, but he didn't care. Courtney had a session with her occupational therapist at one o'clock, and Striker wanted to make damn sure she got there on time.

They parked out front on Camosun Street and Striker got out. High overhead, the sun was bright. The frost on the trees glistened and the lawn looked freshly wet. Everything *shimmered* in the sun. The day felt refreshed. Like spring was on its way.

It made Striker feel good.

He walked up the porch steps into his home. The moment they were inside, Felicia walked over and put on the gas fire, then crashed down on the couch. She draped a blanket over her legs.

'Make yourself comfortable,' he said.

She stretched her arms above her head and let out a yawn. 'Done.'

He was about to join her on the couch, maybe even grab himself a beer – why not? He had earned it – when Courtney exited her bedroom and stepped into the hall on her crutches. She ambled down the hallway, reached him and gave him a one-armed hug.

'Hey, Dad,' she said.

'Hey, Pumpkin. How're the braces holding?'

She gave him an irritated look. 'I've told you before, Dad. They're not braces, they're—'

'A *walker*?'

For a moment, Courtney's eyes took on a resigned look, then her lips crooked into a smile. She leaned over and punched him on the shoulder.

'You're a jerk,' she said.

'I know, but I love ya.'

She smiled at him, and Striker loved to see that. It made him feel good. She was happy.

Then he noticed something else about her. She was dressed in a black pair of Lululemon yoga pants and a dark red workout top that was so tight it looked like a second skin. Bright red lipstick turned her thin lips thick and pouty, and dark eyeliner made her blue eyes stand out like they were coloured contacts. Even her hair was done. Flat-ironed straight.

'Kinda dolled up for therapy,' he noted.

Courtney shared a smirk with Felicia and, as if on cue, the front doorbell rang. When Striker started for the door, Courtney cut him off and gave him a look of daggers.

'*I'll* get it,' she said.

Striker let her. When she opened the door, a young man stood there. He was dressed in casual pants and a Peabody coat. Within two minutes, Striker learned that his name was Jeremy Holmes, he was taking graphic design at BCIT, he was giving Courtney a ride to therapy, and he drove a yellow electric Smartcar.

Before Striker could question the kid further, Courtney intervened. She got between them and ushered Jeremy out through the door. She looked back over her shoulder and grinned as they went.

'Bye, guys. Don't wait up.'

'Goodbye, Pumpkin,' Striker said.

He stood in the doorway, and Felicia joined him. They watched Courtney and her friend approach his car. Once there, Jeremy opened the passenger door for Courtney, took her crutches, helped her inside, and closed the door behind her. He looked back at the house, and gave Striker and Felicia a wave before climbing inside the vehicle.

'I don't like him,' Striker said. 'He has an attitude.'

Felicia grinned. 'You don't like him because he wants your daughter.'

'That's reason enough.'

She squeezed his arm. 'Just be happy she's found someone, and he seems like a nice kid. He certainly doesn't come across like a *bad boy.*'

Striker stared at the small car fading down the road. 'I guess not a lot of bad boys drive yellow Smartcars.'

'Definitely not.' She leaned back and looked at him. 'What did you drive when you were his age?'

'A Volkswagen van.'

'So *you* were the one fathers had to worry about.'

'This isn't about me.'

'It's karma,' she said, and laughed.

Striker grinned at her comment. But he didn't move from the spot. Not even after the little yellow Smartcar had turned the corner and disappeared from view behind the row of houses that lined 29th Avenue.

'It feels like she's growing up too fast,' he said.

'Just be grateful that she can grow up, Jacob. She was a pretty lucky girl last year. It could have turned out far worse.'

Striker nodded in agreement. The words were so true.

One Hundred and Nine

They walked from Camosun up to Dunbar Street, a small stretch of road that owned everything from a Starbucks coffee at 18th Avenue to the movie theatre off 29th. Striker didn't much care where they went. He just wanted to get out of the house.

Having Felicia there with him was an added bonus.

They stopped at an old English pub for lunch and a couple of drinks. Felicia had chicken strips and a glass of red; Striker ordered Toad in the Hole and a tall glass of Guinness. When the draught came, it was dark as molasses and had a swirling cloud of head at the top.

Striker took a long sip of it and felt his body relax.

'So,' Felicia asked. 'How comes the report?'

Striker gave her a weary look. 'I'm hoping to be done by February – of next year.'

She laughed at that. And from there, the conversation jumped all over the place: the possibility of Gabriel not standing trial due to his state of mind; Dalia, missing and still out there somewhere; Larisa recovering nicely; and the monkey court they were going to have to go through over Billy Mercury's death. The one thing they didn't talk about was *them*. And Striker left the topic alone. It was sunny out. He had Felicia with him. And a tall glass of Guinness in his hand.

Why risk ruining that?

As if sensing his thoughts, Felicia reached out and touched his hand. 'You did a good job out there, Jacob, a really good job.'

'We *both* did,' he said. 'We do this stuff together. We're a team, Feleesh.'

The comment made her smile. 'It was a good investigation. Though I have to admit, the best part was the way you led Bernard out to Laroche's place.' She laughed so hard she almost spilled her wine. 'God, that was the best part of the day. You really fooled him.'

Striker was pleased with that. 'Oscar performance?'

'A Golden Globe, at least.'

'A *Globe*? That's an insult.'

'Okay, maybe one of those Emmys then.'

Striker put on his best dejected look, and Felicia grinned back. 'You know, I'm not really all that hungry,' she said. 'If we watch our time, we can get back to your place before Courtney's even left the doctor's office – then I'll give you your real award.'

'On second thoughts, I'll take the Emmy.'

Felicia laughed, and Striker ordered the bill. After he had paid it, he went to get up from the table, but stopped when he saw the intense look Felicia was giving him.

'What?' he asked.

'Where do we go from here, Jacob?'

'Who knows, Feleesh?' he said. 'Just roll the dice.'

Sean Slater
THE SURVIVOR

It's every cop's worst nightmare. Especially when his daughter's in the line of fire.

In his first hour back from a six-month leave of absence, Detective Jacob Striker's day quickly turns into a nightmare when he encounters an Active Shooter situation at his daughter's high school. Three men wearing hockey masks – Black, White, and Red – have stormed the school with firearms and are killing indiscriminately.

Striker takes immediate action. Within minutes two of the gunmen are dead, and Striker is close to ending the violence. But then the last gunman, Red Mask, does something unexpected. He runs up to his fallen comrade, racks the shotgun, and unloads five rounds, obliterating the man's face and hands. And before Striker can react, Red Mask escapes.

Against the clock, Striker investigates the killings for which there is no known motive and no known suspect. Soon his investigation takes him to darker places, and he realizes that not everything at Saint Patrick's High is as it seems. The closer he gets to the truth, the more dangerous his world becomes. Until Striker himself is in the line of fire.

ISBN 978-1-84983-214-4